KU-180-780

ABERDEEN
CITY LIBRARIES
www.aberdeencity.gov.uk/libraries

Cornhill Library
Tel: 01224 696209

It was too late.

She'd seen him. For the first time since she'd walked out of his hospital room. Twenty-six months ago. That had been the last time the world had seen Leonid, too. He'd dropped off the radar completely.

But he was back. Everywhere Kassandra turned there'd been news of him. She'd managed not to look. Until now.

Now her retinas burned with the image of him striding out of his Fifth Avenue headquarters. In spite of herself, she'd strained to see how much of the Leonid she'd known had survived.

The man she'd known had crackled with irrepressible vitality, a smile of whimsy and assurance always hovering on his lips and sparking in his eyes.

The man who'd filled the screen had appeared totally detached, as if he didn't consider himself part of the world anymore. Or as if it was beneath his notice.

And the stalking swagger was gone. In its place was a deliberate, menacing prowl. Whether or not the changes were by-products of the impact of his accident, it had been clear, even in those fleeting moments on-screen:

This wasn't the man she'd known.

* * *

Twin Heirs to His Throne
is part of Mills & Boon Desire's № 1 bestselling series, Billionaires and Babies: Powerful men… wrapped around their babies' little fingers.

TWIN HEIRS
TO HIS THRONE

BY
OLIVIA GATES

First published in Great Britain 2016
By Mills & Boon, an imprint of HarperCollins*Publishers*
1 London Bridge Street, London, SE1 9GF

© 2016 Olivia Gates

ISBN: 978-0-263-26350-3

Our policy is to use papers that are natural, renewable and recyclable
products and made from wood grown in sustainable forests. The logging
and manufacturing processes conform to the legal environmental
regulations of the country of origin.

Printed and bound in Great Britain
by CPI Antony Rowe, Chippenham, Wiltshire

Olivia Gates has always pursued creative passions such as singing and handicrafts. She still does, but only one of her passions grew gratifying enough, consuming enough, to become an ongoing career—writing.

She is most fulfilled when she is creating worlds and conflicts for her characters, then exploring and untangling them bit by bit, sharing her protagonists' every heart-wrenching heartache and hope, their every heart-pounding doubt and trial, until she leads them to an indisputably earned and gloriously satisfying happy ending.

When she's not writing, she is a doctor, a wife to her own alpha male, and a mother to one brilliant girl and one demanding Angora cat. Visit Olivia at oliviagates.com.

Prologue

"**O**nly family is allowed to visit Mr. Voronov, Ms. Stavros."

"At least…"

The nurse cut Kassandra's protest off, stonewalling her again. "Only family is allowed to learn information about his condition."

"But…"

Refusing to give concessions they both knew she wasn't allowed to grant, the nurse rushed away, dismissing her like everyone else had. For the past damned week. Since his accident.

The dread and desperation she'd been struggling to keep at bay rose until she felt her blood charring.

Leonid. Lying somewhere in this hospital, injured, out of reach, with her deprived of even knowing his condition. She wasn't family. She was nothing to him, not to the rest of the world. Nobody knew of their year-long affair.

With no one left to approach for information or reassurance, she staggered to the hectic waiting area of the highest-ranking New York City university hospital. The moment she slumped down on the first vacant seat, the tears she'd been forbidding herself to shed since she'd heard of his accident spilled right out of her soul.

Nothing could happen to him. Her vital, powerful Leonid. She couldn't live without him, could barely remember her life before she'd first laid eyes on him three years ago.

That night, she'd been the star model and one of the top designers in a charity fashion show. As she'd walked out onto the catwalk, her gaze, which normally never focused on anyone in the audience, had been dragged toward a point at the end of the massive space. Then another unprecedented thing had happened. She'd almost stumbled, had stopped for endless, breathless moments, staring at him across the distance, overwhelmed by his sheer gorgeousness and presence.

Though tycoon gods populated her Greek-American family, and she moved in the circles of the megarich and powerful, Leonid was in a league of one. Not only was he a billionaire with a sports-brand empire, but a decathlon world champion…and royalty to boot. He was a prince of Zorya, a kingdom once part of the former Soviet Union, and annexed to Belarus since its disintegration. Though the kingdom hadn't existed in over ninety years, he was still considered royalty in Asia and Europe—and sports and financial royalty in the rest of the world.

Not that any of these attributes had contributed to

his being the only man to ever get her hot and flustered with a mere look. He'd continued to scorch her with such looks for two endless years as they'd moved in the same circles. But nothing had come of it. He'd never come closer than the minimum it had taken him to keep her inflamed and in suspense, until she'd believed that the lust she'd felt blasting from him had been wishful thinking on her part.

Then had come the wedding of one of her best friends, Caliope Sarantos, to Maksim Volkov in Russia. Leonid had been one of the groom's guests. After every man but him had asked her to dance, frustrated out of her mind, she'd escaped outside to get some air. She'd found none when he'd followed her, at last, and taken away her breath completely.

She'd since relived those heart-pounding moments endless times, as he'd closed in on her, informing her that she could no longer run from him. Closing her eyes now, she could again feel his arms around her and his lips over hers as he'd dragged her into that kiss that had made her realize why she hadn't ever let another near. Because she'd been waiting for him her whole life.

But before he'd taken her on what had turned out to be a magical roller-coaster ride, he'd made his intentions clear: nothing but passion and pleasure would be on offer. And Kassandra had been perfectly okay with that. At thirty, she'd never wanted to marry, and she'd long given up on meeting a man she could want, let alone that completely. Finding Leonid had added a totally unexpected and glorious dimension to her life. Having him free from expectations had been a sure path to ecstasy and a surefire guard against disappointment.

Being with him had exhilarated and satisfied her

in ways she hadn't known existed. They'd meshed in every way, met when their hectic schedules allowed, away from the world's eyes, always starving for one another. Keeping their relationship secret from everyone, above all her conservative Greek family who'd long disapproved of her unconventional lifestyle, had made everything even more incendiary.

Then Leonid's training for his upcoming championship had intensified, and between that and running his business empire, she'd seen less and less of him. Media scrutiny had made it impossible to even visit him while he'd trained.

That was when she'd realized she was no longer content with their status quo. But before she'd had time to ponder how to demand a change in the terms of their relationship, he'd had his accident.

From the media reports that had hailed him as a hero, she'd learned that a trailer had flown over the center divider of the I-95 heading into NYC, and into the incoming traffic. Before it had managed to pulverize a car carrying a father and his daughter, Leonid had smashed into their car's side, ramming them out of the path of destruction. But the trailer had slammed into his car full force, catapulting his vehicle into a tumbling crash.

She'd almost fainted with horror at the sight of the crumpled wreck his car had become. It was a miracle he had come out alive.

Desperate to be by his side the moment she'd heard the news, the nightmare had only escalated when she hadn't been able to determine where he'd been taken. Now that she'd finally found him, she'd again been denied any information. She was being treated like the stranger everyone thought she was. He was her lover.

And the father of the baby she'd just yesterday found out she was carrying.

Suddenly, her heart boomed. Was that…?

Yes, yes it was. Ryan McFadden. Her old college friend who'd gone on to become a doctor. She'd seen him a couple of years ago, but he'd been working at another hospital at the time. Finding him here was a lifeline.

Before Ryan could express surprise at seeing her, she flung herself at him, begged him to let her see Leonid, or at least to let her know how he was.

Clearly used to dealing with frantic people, Ryan covered the hands clawing his arm. "I know that apart from his time in surgery, he's been conscious since they brought him in."

He was? And he hadn't called her?

But what if… "C-can he talk?"

"Oh, yes. None of his injuries involved vital organs, thankfully."

And he hadn't left instructions to let her in, or to even let her know how he was?

At her deepening dismay, Ryan rushed on. "He was transferred to an exclusive wing with only his medical team allowed in, to guard against media infringement. But I'll gain access to him. If he grants you permission to visit him…"

"He will." She hugged him fervently. "Thank you."

Giving her a bolstering grin, Ryan strode away.

After what felt like forever, he returned, giving her two thumbs up. She found herself flying to him, so he could take her to Leonid.

At the wing's door, Ryan stopped her. "Listen, Kass, I know it's hard for you to do in your current condition, but keep it light and short, for his sake."

Nodding, she wiped away the tears that had gathered in her eyes again. "How...how bad are his injuries?"

"I don't know details, but when he was brought in I heard he'd suffered compound fractures to both his legs."

Her heart imploded all over again. His legs.

To anyone else, it would mean months of limited mobility. To Leonid, it meant his plans for a new world record were over, who knew for how long. Maybe he'd never heal enough to compete on that elite level again. When that was a major part of his being...

Stop it. She couldn't consider worst-case scenarios. Ryan was right. She had to suppress her own anxiety. Leonid needed her support for the first time ever, and she was damned if she would fail him. Putting on a brave face, she opened the door.

He was the first thing she saw as she stepped into the exquisite suite. Only the bed with monitors surrounding it at its far end betrayed its presence in a medical facility.

Leonid, her beloved lion. He lay sprawled on his back, his perfect body swathed in a hospital gown, already diminished, both legs in full casts, arms limp at his sides, eyes closed. His almost shoulder-length hair lay tousled around a face that was unscathed, but his skin was drained of its normal vital bronze color.

Her heart lurched violently, as if to fling her across the room to him, catapulting her feet forward.

As she eagerly bent to kiss his clamped lips, he opened his eyes. Instead of the most vivid blue, they were almost black. And they slammed into her with the force of a shove. But it was what filled them that had her jackknifing up. Her nerves jangled; her balance wavered. She couldn't be reading the aversion in his expression correctly.

But what gripped his face didn't look like pain, or the effect of a drug. There was no distress or fogginess in his eyes, just clarity and…emptiness.

Telling herself it was an expected by-product of everything he'd gone through, she reached for his hand, suppressed a shudder at how cold it was. "Leonid, darling…"

He tugged his hand away, harder than necessary, from her trembling hold. "I'm fine."

Reminding herself that what she felt didn't matter, that only he did, she forced a smile. "You do look…"

His glacial look stopped her flimsy lie in its tracks. "I know how I look. But I *am* fine, considering." A beat. "I hear you kicked up quite a commotion trying to get to me."

He knew? And he hadn't told them to let her in earlier?

His expression became even more inanimate as he looked away. "I kept hoping you'd give up and just leave."

Her throat squeezed, making it nearly impossible to breathe. "I—I realize how you must feel. But there will be other championships…"

He cut her off again. "I'm sick of people placating me."

Telling herself he needed her nearness even if his current mood made him pretend he didn't, she sat down and caressed his corded forearm, trying to infuse him with her strength and let their connection bolster him. "I'm not 'people,' Leonid. I'm your woman, your lover, and you're my…"

His gaze swung to hers, this time filled with frost. "You're free to consider yourself whatever you want, but I'm certainly not your anything."

The lump in her throat grew spikes. But still convinced it was his ordeal talking, she tried again. "Leonid, darling…"

He shook off her hand, his face twisting in a snarl. "Don't you dare 'darling' me. I made my terms clear from the start. The only reason I was with you was because I thought you agreed to them."

Shocked out of her wits at his viciousness, she again told herself she must have gravely underestimated the effects of his injuries and near-death experience, that it was better to withdraw now, before he got even more worked up.

She stood up carefully so she wouldn't sway. "I only wanted to know you're okay… I shouldn't have disturbed you…"

"No, you shouldn't have. But now I'm glad you did."

"Y-you are?"

"That's the one good thing that's come out of this mess. It's giving me the chance to do what I've been trying to do."

Her heart decelerated, as if afraid to beat and let his meaning sink in. "What have you been trying to do?"

"I've been trying to end this."

Her heart stopped. "This? You mean…us?"

His stone-cold gaze slammed into her, compromising what was left of her balance. "There was never an 'us.' I thought we had an arrangement for sexual recreation, to unwind from the stresses of the pursuits that matter in our lives. But you were only pretending to abide by my terms, until I was softened enough, or maybe weakened enough, as you must believe I am now, to change the terms to what you wanted all along, weren't you? You're just another status-hunting, biological-clock-ticking woman after all, aren't you?"

Unable to breathe, she flinched away. "Please…stop…"

He pushed a button that brought him to a seated position, as if to pursue her to drive his point through her heart. "I'm not stopping until this is over, once and for all. I grabbed the opportunity of training to break it off with you naturally, but you only escalated your pursuit. And now that you think me a sitting duck, you're here to pin me down? To smother me with solicitude at my lowest ebb? You think you'll make me so grateful I'll end up offering you a commitment?"

She shook her head, shook all over, the tears she'd suppressed burning from her depths again. "You know it was never like that. Please, just calm down…"

"So now you want to make it look as if I'm raving and ranting? But you're right. I'm not calm. I'm fed up. What else can I do so you'll understand I can't bear your suffocating sweetness anymore?"

Shock seeping deeper into her marrow, she staggered back to escape his mutilating barrage. "Please… enough… I'll leave…"

"And you won't return. Ever."

His icy savagery shredded her insides. It was as if the man she loved had never existed. As if the accident had only revealed the real him, someone who relished employing cruelty to get rid of what he considered a nuisance.

She'd swayed halfway to the door before she stopped.

She couldn't bear telling him. It would only validate his accusations. But he had to know.

Teetering around, she met the baleful bleakness of his stare, and forced the admission out. "I—I'm pregnant."

Something spiked in his gaze before his thick lashes lowered, and he seemed to be contemplating something horrific.

At length, demeanor emptied of all expression, he raised his gaze to her. "Are you considering keeping it?"

Her world tilted. The Leonid she'd known would have never asked this. The real Leonid did because it was clear he'd rather she didn't.

Trying to postpone falling apart until she walked out, she choked, "I only told you because I thought you had a right to know. I guess you would have rather not known."

"Answer me."

The remaining notches of her control slipped. "Why are you asking?" she cried. "You made it clear you care nothing about what I do or about me at all."

He held her gaze, the nothingness in his eyes engulfing her.

Then he just said, "I don't."

One

Two years later...

"After his disappearance from public view over two years ago, Prince Leonid Voronov is back in the spotlight. The former decathlon world champion dropped off the radar after suffering injuries in a car crash that took him off the competitive circuits. Now the billionaire founder and CEO of Sud, named after the Slavic god of destiny and glory, one of the largest multinational corporations of sports apparel, equipment, accessories and services, could be poised to become much more. As one of three contenders for the resurrected throne of Zorya, a nation now in the final stages of seceding from Belarus, he could soon become king. With our field reporter on the scene as the former sports royalty and possible future king exited his New York headquarters..."

Kassandra fumbled for the remote, pushing every button before she managed to turn off the TV just as Leonid appeared on the screen.

But it was too late. She'd seen him. For the first time since she'd walked out of his hospital room twenty-six months ago. That had been the last time the world had seen him, too. He'd dropped off the radar completely ever since.

But he was back. Reentering the world yesterday like a meteor, making everyone gape in wonder as he hurtled out of nothingness, burning brighter than ever.

Everywhere she'd turned in the past twenty-four hours there'd been news of him. She'd avoided getting swept up in the tide of the world's curiosity about his reappearance, at least outwardly. Until now.

Now her retinas burned with the image of him striding out of his imposing Fifth Avenue headquarters. In spite of herself, she'd strained to see how much of the Leonid she'd known had survived his abrupt retirement from his life's passion.

The man she'd known had been crackling with vitality, a smile of whimsy and assurance always hovering on his lips and sparkling in the depths of his eyes. He'd perpetually looked aware of everything and everyone surrounding him, always connected and tapping in to the fabric of energy that made the world. She'd always felt as if he was always ready to break out in a run and overtake everyone as easily as he breathed. Which he'd literally done for eight years straight.

The man who'd filled the screen had appeared to be totally detached, as if he no longer was part of the world anymore. Or as if it was beneath his notice.

And there'd been another change. The stalking swagger was gone. In its place was a deliberate, almost menacing prowl. Whether this and the other changes she'd observed were sequels of the physical or psychological impact of his accident, one thing was clear, even in those fleeting moments.

This wasn't the man she'd known.

Or rather, the man she'd thought she'd known.

She'd long faced the fact that she'd known nothing of him. Not before she'd been with him, or while they'd been together, or after he'd shoved her away and vanished.

For most of that time, Kassandra had withdrawn from the world, too. After the shock of his rejection, she'd drowned in despondence as its implications and those of her pregnancy had sunk in. She'd been pathetic enough to be literally sick with worry about him, to pine for him until she'd wasted away. Until she'd almost miscarried.

That scare had finally jolted her to the one reality she'd been certain of. That she'd wanted that baby with everything in her and would never risk losing it. That day at the doctor's, she'd found out she wasn't carrying one baby, but two.

After the scare and the discovery, she'd forced everything into perspective, then had even progressed to consider what had happened a blessing. Before Leonid, she'd never thought she'd get married. She'd never considered marriage an option between them, not even when she'd wanted to demand a change in their arrangement. But she'd always wanted to be a mother. Especially after her best friends, Selene, Caliope and Naomi, had had their children. She'd known she wanted what they had, that she'd be good at it, that it would complete her life.

As he'd said, one good thing had come out of that

mess. She would be a mother without the complication of having a man around.

Not that it had been smooth sailing. Being pregnant and alone after the unbearable emotional injury of his rejection had been the hardest thing she'd ever gone through. Her family hadn't made it any easier. Their first reactions had ranged from mortification to outrage. Her mother had lamented that she'd deprived her of the traditional Greek wedding she'd planned for her from childhood, while her father had swung between wrathfully demanding the name of the bastard who'd impregnated and abandoned her to forbidding her to have a baby out of wedlock. Her siblings and other relatives had had a combination of both reactions to varying degrees, even those who'd tried to be progressive and supportive.

The only ones who'd been fully behind her from day one had been her trio of close friends. Not only had they always been there for her and vice versa, no questions asked, they'd once been in her situation. Even if *their* stories had progressed toward ecstatic endings.

But when her family realized the price for any negative stance would be never seeing her again, they'd relented. Their disappointment and misgivings had gradually melted, especially her parents', giving way to full involvement in her pregnancy and the preparation for her delivery. After the twins had arrived, they'd become everyone's favorites and considered to be the best thing that had ever happened to Kassandra. Everything had worked out for the best.

She'd reclaimed herself and her stability, had become even more successful career-wise, but most important she'd become a mother to two perfect daughters. Eva and Zoya. She'd given them both names meaning life, as they'd given *her* new life.

Then Zorya had suddenly filled the news with a declaration of its intention to reinstate the monarchy. With every rapid development, foreboding had filled her. Even when she'd had no reason to think it would make Leonid resurface.

It seemed her instincts had been correct, for here he was, back on the scene with a vengeance. In one day, he'd taken the world by storm, a mystic figure rising from the ashes of oblivion like a phoenix.

Leonid's disappearance had been the one thing left unresolved inside her. Everything she'd ever felt for or because of him had long dissipated. But wondering where he'd gone and what he'd been up to had lingered. Now explanations would be unearthed and any remaining mystique surrounding him would be gone, so she could once again resume her comforting routines, untouched by his disruption.

Leonid was a page that hadn't only been turned, but burned.

"Mama."

The tension clamping her every muscle suddenly drained at the chirping call of her eldest-by-minutes daughter, Eva. The girls had started calling her Mama two months ago. She hadn't thought it would be that big of a deal. But every time they said it, which was often now that they knew it activated her like nothing else, another surge of sheer love and indulgence flooded her. Her lips spread with delight as she strode through her spacious, cheerfully decorated Bel Air house to their room.

It had been like this for months. Eva and Zoya always woke up an hour after she put them to bed. It was as if they loathed wasting precious playtime sleeping, or thought they shouldn't leave her alone. But since she'd gone back to work after their first birthday almost six months ago, and they spent mornings with Kyria Despina, her late uncle's wife and now her nanny, she welcomed the extra time with them.

As she approached the nursery, she could hear the girls' efforts to climb out of their cribs through the ajar door. They were able to do it after a few trials now, but would soon be experts at it. She debated whether to go in or to let them complete their task and toddle their way to her in their playroom, as she'd been doing lately. It was why she'd been leaving the door ajar. She had child-proofed every inch of her home six thousand ways from Sunday after all.

Moments passed and neither toddler showed up at the end of the corridor. Heart booming with the always-hovering anxiety she'd learned was a permanent side effect of motherhood, she streaked inside and found both girls standing in their crib, literally asleep on their feet.

The tenacious tots were obeying their regular programming even though their strenuously fun weekend at Disneyland had left them wiped out.

Scooping them up, she held one in each arm in the way she'd perfected, cooing to them, letting them know as they nestled into her and made those sweet sleep sounds that she'd come, as she always would, that they hadn't missed that extra time with her they'd wanted.

Once she laid them down again, each turned to her favorite position and resumed a deep, contented sleep.

Sighing at that tremor of acute love and gratitude coursing through her, she walked out, closing the door completely now that she knew they were down for the night.

The moment she exited the room, the doorbell rang.

Frowning, she remembered that the girls' play pals, Judy and Mikey, had again left behind some toys she'd found only after a thorough tidying up. It had become a ritual for Sara, their mother and her neighbor, to come by and collect her children's articles after she'd put them to bed. They usually ended up having a cup of tea to unwind together after their hectic days.

Rushing to the door, she opened it with a ready smile. "We should establish rules about allowing only in-house toys..."

Air clogged her lungs. All her nerves fired, short-circuiting her every muscle, especially her heart.

Leonid.

Right there. On her doorstep.

She'd visualized this encounter countless times in waking trances and suffocating dreams. The perverse yearning had risen time and again for him to show up, look down at her from his prodigious height with eyes full of all he'd deprived her of, and tell her everything that had happened since his accident had been a terrible dream. She'd hoped for it until hope had turned to ashes.

And now...out of the blue, he was here...

Oh, God! He is really here.

Almost unrecognizable. Yet distressingly the same.

Observations accumulated in the white noise that filled her mind, burying her. The most obvious change was his hair. The silk that had been long enough to wind around her hands in the throes of passion was now severely cropped. It still suited him. It actually suited him better, accentuating the dominance of his bone structure.

The other major difference was his body. It hadn't been a distortion of the video or his size relative to others. He *was* bigger. Broader. More heavily muscled. The leanness of the runner had been replaced by the bulk of a supreme fitness athlete.

His every feature and nuance, familiar yet radically different, felt like a knife to the heart.

But on the whole, he looked as if everything human about him had melted away, revealing a creature of polished steel beneath. Even the way he held himself seemed…inhuman. As if he was now a being of pure intellect and purpose, like a cyborg, an animate form of artificial intelligence.

An hour could have passed as she gaped up at him and he stared blankly down at her. He'd always had that power. Time had always distorted when she'd entered his orbit.

"Invite me in, Kassandra."

His bottomless voice yanked her out of the stupor she'd stumbled in.

"I will do no such thing."

"Your porch isn't the place for what I've come to say."

Her mouth dropped open at his audacity. That he could just appear on her doorstep after what he'd done to her, and without even an attempt at apology or even civility, not only demand but expect to be invited in.

"There's no place where you can say anything to me. We have absolutely nothing to say to each other."

"After the past two years, we have plenty."

"The past two years are exactly why there's nothing to be said. Even if there was, I'm not interested in hearing it."

His eyes gave her a clinical sweep, as if assessing her

response for veracity and judging it to be false. It made her loathe her weakness for him all over again.

"I don't know what you were thinking coming here like this, what you expected, but if…"

"If you're still angry, we can discuss that, too."

If? *If?*

"Are you sure you broke only your legs in that accident? Sounds as if you'd pulverized way more. Like the components that made you human."

"I do realize showing up here must have surprised you…"

"Try *appalled* and *outraged.*"

He shifted, like the automaton she'd just accused him of becoming, as if moving into a different gear to counter her response. "That's why I showed up. I gathered if I called ahead, you would have been just as resistant to granting me an audience. So I decided to eliminate unnecessary steps."

"And this single step turned out to be as pointless. I'm not granting you an audience since we have zero things to discuss, so you might as well save us both the aggravation and go disappear again. Preferably forever this time."

"If you're concerned I might be here to exhume the past, rest assured I have no wish to resurrect anything between us. I'm not here for you at all. I'm here for my daughters."

Every word sank into her mind like a depth mine. Then the last ones exploded.

I'm here for my daughters.

My daughters.

The rage that detonated inside her, that he would dare say this, or even think it, almost rocked her on her feet.

Biting a tongue that had gone numb with fury, she gritted out, "Leave. Right this second."

Unperturbed, he gave a nonchalant shrug of his daunting shoulder. "I will leave after I've said what I came to say and when we've come to a preliminary understanding. Whether you approve or not, I am the father of your twin daughters, and I am here to—"

Red smeared her vision. "You won't be here much longer or I'm calling the police."

His searing blue gaze remained still, his pupils unmoving, indicating he had no emotional response to her threat and agitation. "I would advise against this. It would disrupt your neighborhood and bring you unneeded speculation and embarrassment. Not to mention you'd have to lie to the police to make them take action against me…"

"I won't be lying when I say you're here uninvited, harassing me and making fraudulent claims to *my* daughters."

"They're my daughters, too."

"Not according to the law, they're not. Nor to them or to the whole world. Any passing stranger they've ever briefly met is more to them than you are."

His formidable head inclined in agreement. "I know that being their biological father on its own means nothing. That's why I'm here, and I'm not going anywhere until I say my piece or until you indicate your willingness to negotiate further."

"What the hell do you mean, negotiate?"

"Over the twins, of course."

She gaped, unable to voice any of the million violent protests ricocheting in her skull and boiling her blood.

"Before you blast me off the face of the earth, I remind you that as their biological father, I do have a right to—"

"You have absolutely no right to Eva and Zoya. None. You relinquished any right to even think of them as yours way before they were born. You made it clear you didn't even want them to be born. You may have forgotten this, but I remember all too well."

"I freely admit I behaved extremely…inappropriately when you came to me after my accident. You can understand I was at my worst at the time."

"And you remained there for over two years?"

"I'm the first to admit it took me longer than acceptable to deal with everything."

Rage deepening at his dismissal of his abandonment of her, she seethed, "I care nothing about why you did what you did, and I'll be damned if I let you pretend it was forgivable and invade my life again. You're sure as hell never coming near my daughters."

"I'm not here seeking forgiveness. I don't waste my time, and I certainly won't waste yours pursuing the unattainable. But I'm here to acknowledge my responsibilities. Whatever I've done, I'm myself again."

"If you think *that* makes it any better, let me disabuse you of that notion. Being yourself is proof you know nothing of responsibility or accountability or even common courtesy and basic humanity."

Instead of stonewalling her again, he just nodded impassively. "You're right. My old self was nothing to be proud of. But the past couple of years changed me, and the man I am today is capable of at least being fully responsible and accountable, and resolved to take on his duties."

"Good for 'him.' And as long as 'he' takes his resolutions away from my family, I wish 'him' the best of luck."

"The thing is, your family is also mine. The twins are the primary duty I'm determined to take on."

She fought harder against the screams gathering at the back of her throat. "That would have been a commendable sentiment if they needed anything from you. Which they don't. And they never will. You've done your part and can now feel proud of yourself when you leave and never come back."

His azure gaze remained unwavering. "I do understand your alarm and rejection. But even if the past was rife with pain, I'm certain everything happened for a reason. Why else would I have twin girls, and now be called on to take the mantle of responsibility in the land of the twin goddesses?"

This made zero sense to her, leaving her speechless again.

Realizing she had no ready comeback, he straightened even more, seeming to grow bigger, more rigid and imposing. "I won't push for this audience tonight. I'll give you some time. Not long but enough to let it all sink in."

And a croak finally escaped her. "Let what sink in?"

"The fact that I am back to stay. That nothing will stop me from claiming my throne, and my heirs."

Two

Kassandra's entranced gaze followed Leonid as he descended the stairs of her porch, then crossed her driveway in measured strides to his parked car, a gleaming black Jaguar that looked like an extension of him.

Without looking back, he got in and drove away slowly, almost soundlessly. After the car disappeared, she remained staring at the void it had left, her mind a debris field in the wake of the havoc he'd wreaked.

Had he really been here? Or had she conjured him after seeing him earlier in that news spot? Had it all been a dream, a nightmare?

But if it had been, why couldn't she wake up, as she always did whenever his phantasm came to suffocate her at night? As much as she would have preferred an actual breakdown to him being here, she knew. He had been here. And he would be back. His last words rang in her ears in an unending loop.

Nothing will stop me from claiming my throne, and my heirs.

Legs trembling with futile rage and incipient dread, she closed the door. But it was no use. She didn't feel she'd successfully shut him out, or that she was safe anymore inside her home.

As she shakily made her way inside, one thing he'd said buzzed into her brain like an electric drill.

Why else would I have twin girls, and now be called on to take the mantle of responsibility in the land of the twin goddesses?

What had *that* meant?

She had to find out. Her first priority was to understand the motive behind his sudden interest in Eva and Zoya. Knowledge would be her best weapon against his unexpected incursion.

Still unsteady, she got some water and headed to her home office. She sat down at her desk and opened her laptop. After staring at the search engine numbly for several moments, she typed in *Zorya*.

For hours, she read all there was to read about the mythology behind that name and the land that wielded it.

It turned out Zorya was a plural name, incorporating the two guardian goddesses, Zarya and Zvezda, who represented the morning and evening stars. According to Slavic mythology, they were charged through eternity with guarding the doomsday hound, Simargi, lest he consumed the constellation Ursa Minor. They were also responsible for opening and closing the gates for the sun. Zorya, the former—and soon to be again—kingdom was said to be the only place where both stars could be perpetually seen on all clear nights. Its coat of arms depicted the blonde and dark-haired goddesses holding up stars. Though the goddesses were twins, they were quite literally night and day.

Just like her girls.

Eva had taken after her, Zoya after Leonid.

So this was what he'd meant. He considered this a sign he was meant to have both the throne and the girls.

And she'd seen it in his eyes.

He would make it all come true.

After an oppressive night spent pondering every possible distressing outcome of Leonid's reappearance, Kassandra struggled to perform her morning rituals with the girls before leaving them with Kyria Despina and heading to work. Not that she expected to get any work done, but she needed to be away from them. She'd be damned if she'd let Leonid poison their moods, too.

In half an hour, she was in her personal office on the second floor of her company, looking out the window at downtown LA but only seeing the chaos inside her mind.

What disturbed her most was that she hadn't come up with a plan of action in case Leonid *did* pursue his objectives. Which she had no doubt he would.

"I'm sorry, Kass, I tried to…"

Even before her PA's cut-short exclamation, Kassandra's senses had gone haywire.

Swinging around, hoping she was wrong but certain she wasn't, the air was still knocked out of her at the sight of him. Leonid.

He filled her doorway, dwarfing her delicate PA. Mindy was looking up at him with a mixture of mortification and all-out awe.

Kassandra understood. How she did. A god walking the earth wouldn't have looked as imposing and over-powering.

Their gazes collided, almost making her stumble against the plate glass of her wall-to-wall window. It was him who relinquished their visual lock first to look down at Mindy, who resembled a tiny herbivore that found itself in the crosshairs of a great feline.

"I apologize for overriding you, Ms. Levine. Ms. Stavros will fully understand that there was nothing you could have done to stop me. You can rest assured she'll chastise me appropriately for such high-handed behavior."

Gathering what she could of her wits, Kassandra tore her gaze off him and focused on her assistant. "It's okay, Mindy." Mindy looked back as if in a trance. Kassandra sighed. "You can go now, thanks. I'll let you know if I decide to call security."

With a ghost of a smile, Leonid stepped aside to allow Mindy to stumble out. "She won't. You can drop the red alert."

The moment the door closed, Leonid turned his focus to her. It was a good thing she'd moved to her desk so she could mask her own unsteadiness and feign a con-frontational pose.

"Don't be so sure, Leonid. My private security isn't the police and won't care if you broke any laws. The one thing that will matter to them is that I don't want you here."

"How do you know you don't want me here before you hear what I have to say?"

"I already heard it, and I not only would rather you spare me an encore, but I also wish there was some cosmic erase button to have it unsaid. If that's all you're here to say, I will cut everything short and have you removed."

"You don't need to bother. I will remove myself once I've done what I've come to do. And it's not to reiterate what I said last night. I'm here to state my terms."

"This time I will spare myself the aggravation of reacting to your terminal audacity. The answer to anything you have to say is no anyway."

"If you remember anything about me, you should know I do not take no for an answer. Now, more than ever, I won't."

Every nerve jangled as he approached, as if to emphasize that there was no stopping his invasion of her life. With every step, she felt as if he was planting a foothold that she wouldn't be able to uproot.

"My terms are the following—I want to become Eva and Zoya's father, in name and in reality. You will give me full access to them, effective immediately. You won't try to do anything to put them off me, or to put off the procedure of declaring me as their father. I will have them bear my name before the coronation. It is in just over a month's time."

Feeling she'd taken a deep breath underwater, her protest came out a gurgle. "Now, look here…"

He continued as if she hadn't interrupted. "As their mother, you can and will of course dictate your own terms and I will meet every one."

She shook her head, as if to shake off a punch to the face. "My only term is that you get the hell out of my life. You stayed out of it for two years. And that is where I demand you stay."

His face remained as hard as stone. "That is not an option. Anything else is negotiable."

"Nothing else is worth negotiating. I won't let you walk into my life, making those insane demands and expecting me to fall in with your timetable."

"I'm not walking into your life, but my daughters'."

Knowing he was powerful enough to do whatever he wished, her mind burned rubber trying to latch on to an alternative to anger or defiance to hold him at bay. Those had gotten her nowhere. Continuing to challenge him head-on would only make him more intractable. If that was even possible.

Her only way out could be to negotiate a less-damaging deal. Something other than the takeover he was bent on.

"Listen, Leonid, let's take a time-out and rewind to the beginning. Let's say, for whatever reasons, you wish to acknowledge the girls as your daughters. I can, if necessary, live with that. We can come to an agreement where you can be…included. That doesn't mean you have to be in their lives. You haven't been since before they were born and they *are* totally fine without a father. I'm not saying this to be vindictive, or because of our personal history. It's just a fact. Also consider the effort and time commitment that goes into being a parent. You can't possibly want to be a father, especially now that you're on the verge of becoming a king. You literally have far better and more important things to do."

He waited until she finished her speech, then demolished it with that vacant look. "There's nothing better or more important than becoming the father my daughters deserve. And need. No matter how adequate you are as a single parent."

Her rage seethed again. "You know nothing of how

adequate I am as a single parent, or what my daughters need."

"Like you take exception to my opinion of your life, I would appreciate you not passing judgment on mine. Being a father is exactly what I now want to be. Becoming a king only makes it more imperative I claim all my responsibilities with the utmost commitment."

"Fine, I won't presume to know what you want. I'll keep to my side of things. I need no commitment from you."

"Then, I will change your mind about what you need."

The way he'd said that… The way his gaze dropped to envelop her body before returning stonily to hers…

Did…did he mean something personal? Intimate…?

Before her thoughts caught fire, he disabused her of any ridiculous notion this was in any way about her. "No matter how strong, resourceful and successful you are, and though you've been coping exceptionally well being both a mother and a businesswoman, you will experience a huge improvement in the quality of your and the twins' lives when you have me as a fully committed partner in raising them."

She shook her head, feeling punch-drunk. "You come here…and just dictate to me…about the quality of my—"

"I came here, your territory still, but a less personal one, after your reaction to my showing up on your doorstep last night, because I thought you might feel less cornered here. It's also why I didn't have you brought to me."

That made her locate her faltering verbal skills with a vengeance. "Oh, how considerate of you. I should be grateful you didn't have me dragged to your territory, and instead chose to invade my professional space, getting my whole company abuzz with speculation, launching a hundred rumors, undermining me and generally disrupting my life?"

"I figured whatever I did, it wouldn't meet with your approval, so I did what I thought least threatening to you."

"Great rationalization, but..."

He continued speaking as if he was playing back a recording. "Starting tomorrow, I expect to be allowed in to see my daughters without resistance or ill will. I would very much prefer, for their sake and yours, if we do this on the most amicable terms possible. I hope you won't force me to resort to more drastic measures."

Having finished the speech he'd come to deliver, he turned and walked away. She could only stare after him, feeling as if she were sinking in quicksand.

Before he stepped out the door, he paused, turned. "I'll come by your house a couple of hours before the twins' bedtime."

Kassandra waited until he closed the door after him, then collapsed on her chair like a demolished building.

As everything seeped into her mind and its full impact registered, she reeled harder. Not only with the disaster in progress she could see spiraling out of control, but with how much of a stranger he'd become.

Those first hellish months after he'd kicked her out of his life, she'd been anguished by how his feelings for her had withered, then reversed. But with him so distant and clinical now, she finally believed he'd never felt anything in the first place. She didn't count at all to him, neither in the past nor in the future he had so carefully planned for them all.

The future she couldn't let come to pass.

She couldn't let this automaton near her daughters. His new programming might dictate it, but if there was anyone Eva and Zoya were better off without it was him.

But she couldn't stop him. He had the legal and personal clout to do what he wanted. She didn't have a leg to stand on, let alone a weapon to fight him off with.

But…that wasn't true. She did have weapons.

At least her best friends did. Selene, Caliope and Naomi had access to three of the most lethal weapons in the world. Their husbands. Each man was at least as powerful as Leonid was, if not more. He'd have no chance against their combined might.

Fumbling for her cell phone, she called Selene. As soon as she answered, she told her she was adding another call to Caliope, then repeated the process with her, adding another to Naomi, too, merging the calls.

The three women, once they were part of a four-way conference call with her, chorused anxiously, "What's wrong?"

"Everything," she choked. "I need Aristedes. And Maksim. And Andreas."

Six hours later, Kassandra looked around her office, her cheeks burning.

Her friends hadn't even asked her why she'd needed their husbands. After making sure she wasn't in any immediate danger, they'd all hung up. She'd expected them to get their husbands to call. They'd actually sent them over in person.

And here they all were. Aside from Leonid, the three most imposing and hard-hitting men she'd ever seen.

According to Aristedes's concise explanation, as soon as their wives had told them to drop everything and fly to her side, they'd each jumped on their jets and crossed the continent from New York to her. And they didn't seem bothered in the least by being ordered around like that to do her bidding...or rather their wives'. If she didn't love her friends so completely, she would have envied them having such unique men wrapping themselves so lovingly around their every inch. Their fairytale relationships had always emphasized how abysmal her situation with Leonid was.

Loath to impose on them more than absolutely necessary, she rushed to recount her dilemma.

But as she talked, the men looked much like three souls who'd walked into the middle of a foreign movie, clearly lost.

"Hold on a minute." That was Aristedes, shipping magnate and Selene's, her oldest friend's, husband. It had been through Selene's marriage to him that all of them had become best friends. Caliope being Aristedes's sister and Maksim's wife, and Naomi, Selene's sister-in-law and Andreas's wife. He sat forward with a spectacular frown marring his impossibly handsome face. "You're talking about Leonid Voronov?"

She'd confided in her best friends about Leonid when she'd told them of her pregnancy. Since they told their husbands everything, she'd assumed they'd told them. But it was clear, if Aristedes's reaction was any indication, that her friends considered her secrets sacrosanct.

It meant this meeting just got more agonizingly embarrassing, as she had to explain everything from the start.

After she did, Maksim, the one who used to have a personal relationship with Leonid, stood up, rage distorting his equally impressive face. "You mean you told him you were pregnant, and he didn't only kick you out of his life, but implied he'd prefer you terminated your pregnancy?" As she nodded warily, he growled, "*I'm* dealing with that scum of the earth. He's a fellow Russian and it's on me you met him at all. I invited the louse to my wedding."

"Settle down, Maksim." That was Andreas, Aristedes's younger brother and the most dangerous of the lot. "If there's punishment to be doled out, we're all getting a piece of him." He swung his icy gaze to Kassandra, making her almost regret recruiting their help. Andreas had once been involved in organized crime, and remained as lethal, if not more so, now that he'd gone legit. "But this guy says he's back to atone for his mistakes. Any reason to believe he doesn't mean it?"

"Oh, I believe he means it," she groaned. "As much as I believe the road to hell for me and the girls is paved with his good intentions."

Aristedes pursed his lips, propping an elbow on a knee. "But if he's owning up to his responsibilities, perhaps you should give him some leeway, in a limited wait-and-see fashion, without making any promises or changes in your lives?" Aristedes looked first at Maksim and then Andreas. "I think I speak for all of us when I say we were all once in more or less his same position, and we would have given anything for a second chance with the women we love and the children we fathered, or in Andreas's case, the child he was named guardian of."

Maksim's dark fury ebbed as he considered his brother-in-law's point of view. "Now that you put it that way, I can't even think what would have become of me if Caliope hadn't given me a second chance. One I didn't think I deserved and she had every right not to give me at the time."

Heart contracting at the turn in conversation, she choked out, "None of your situations was anything like mine with him."

Maksim winced. "Now that I think of it, I almost did the same thing to Caliope. I, too, abandoned her when I knew she was pregnant."

"It's not the same at all," she protested. Maksim had had the best of reasons for walking away. His father had been abusive. He'd feared he'd inherited his proclivities and had been terrified of hurting his vulnerable loved ones. "You thought you were protecting her and your baby."

Maksim sat back down, gaze gentling. "Maybe he has a valid reason, too? At least one he believed to be valid?"

Feeling cornered, she realized she couldn't get them on board without telling them *everything*. What he'd said to her in the past, and in the present, that she'd never meant a thing to him, that he was only back now for his "heirs" because he believed it was his duty and destiny, now that he was going to be king of the land of the two goddesses.

By the time she'd finished, all three men's faces were closed with so much wrath, she felt anxious about the extreme measures they might take in dealing with Leonid. In spite of everything, she found herself worried for him.

As she tried to think of a way to mitigate their outrage and their consequent actions, Maksim heaved up to his feet again, clearly bringing this meeting to an end.

"Don't worry about Leonid anymore, Kassandra," Maksim said. "I'll deal with him."

Following him up, Andreas corrected, "*We'll* deal with him."

Troubled by the respectively murderous and predatory looks in the two men's eyes, she turned to Aristedes, her oldest acquaintance among them, and ironically, since he was generally known as the devil, the one who scared her the least.

Sensing her anxiety, Aristedes gave her shoulder a bolstering squeeze. "I'll keep those two in check, and resolve this situation with the least damage possible."

As they each gave her pecks on the cheek, she was torn between being alarmed she'd let loose those hounds of hell on Leonid, and being relieved she'd soon have this nightmare over with.

By the time she leaned back on the door, panting as if she'd run a mile, she decided she should be only relieved.

Leonid had only himself to blame for whatever they did to him. If he wanted to escape those men's punishment, he should have settled for being a king, away from her and the girls.

"Yes, I understand," Kassandra said to Maksim.

She'd said almost the same thing to Andreas and Aristedes before him, just to end the calls with them, too.

For she certainly didn't understand at all. How the three predators, who'd left her office out for blood yesterday, had each come back to her less than a day later, purring a totally different tune. That of urging her to give Leonid a chance.

How had he managed to get to them all? What had he said to have them so wholeheartedly on his side?

But why was she even wondering? Didn't she already know how irresistible he could be when he put his mind to it? He'd worked the three men over but good. It was clear that their initial thoughts about having once been in Leonid's shoes and in need of clemency were back in full force. Anything she said now would be her intolerant word against Leonid's penitent one.

Putting down her cell phone, she pressed her fingers against burning eyelids.

So. She was out of options. There was no way she could stop Leonid herself. All she could do now was make sure he didn't turn their lives upside down.

Suddenly, another bolt of agitation zapped her.

The bell. Leonid. He was here. *Exactly* two hours before Eva and Zoya's bedtime, as promised.

She wouldn't even wonder how he knew at what time she put them to bed. She had a sick feeling he knew everything about her life with the girls over the past two years. And that there was far more to this whole thing than he was letting on.

Yet she could do nothing but play along, and see what exactly he wanted, and where this would lead.

Crossing from her home office past the living room, she signaled to Kyria Despina that she'd get the door.

She took her time, but Leonid didn't ring again. Stopping at the door, she could almost feel him on the other side, silently telling her he'd wait out her reluctance and wear down her resistance.

She pressed her forehead against the cool mahogany, gathering her wits and stamina. Then she straightened, filled her lungs with much-needed air and opened the door.

As always, nothing prepared her for laying eyes on him. Every time she ever had, an invisible hand wrapped around her heart and squeezed. Her senses ignited at his nearness, each time more than the time before.

Standing like a monolith on her doorstep, he was swathed in a slate-gray coat, a suit of the same color and a shirt as vivid as his eyes, radiating that inescapable magnetism that had snared her even before she'd laid eyes on him. Blood rushed to her head before flooding her body in scalding torrents.

And she cursed him, and herself, all over again. For him to still have this choke hold over her senses, when he didn't even try, didn't even want to, was the epitome of unfairness. But life was exactly that. As was he. Both did what they wanted to her, her approval irrelevant, her will overruled.

So she'd let him take his invasion to the next level. She only hoped after getting a dose of domesticity, he'd retreat to a nominal position in the girls' lives, which she could deal with without too much damage to herself.

Certain she was opening the door to a new dimension of heartache, she said, "Come in, Leonid."

Three

Leonid crossed Kassandra's threshold.

For a second, before she retreated, he almost touched her. It was the last thing he wanted to do. The one thing he couldn't bear.

If he could have done any of this without seeing her at all, he would have jumped at the chance. But it was out of the question. If he wanted his daughters, she had to be involved. Closely. Suffocatingly.

Mercifully, she'd been averse, keeping him at the distance he needed to remain, in every way. But right now he'd miscalculated his movement, and she hadn't receded fast enough. A second after he'd advanced, their clothes had whispered off each other. Just being near her caused the slow burn in his every nerve to spark into a scalding sizzle.

Before he could judge if the fleeting contact had disturbed her, too, she turned and strode away, leaving him to follow in her wake, a path filled with her sense-warping warmth and scent.

The glance she threw at him over her shoulder spoke volumes, making it even harder to breathe. The surface layer was annoyance that he'd showed up at all, and at the exact time he'd said he would. Then there was resignation that she couldn't turn him away. Beneath that lay another sort of anger he couldn't fathom. And at the core of it all, there was...a threat.

They both knew he wielded power that would give him access to the twins no matter what she did. She'd tried to recruit allies to stop him. She'd picked them well. But after he'd neutralized their threat, she must have realized there was no point in prolonging a losing fight. Being the pragmatic businesswoman that she was, she'd wasted no more time coming to the best course of action. Let him have what he wanted. For now. Until she studied the situation further and decided if she could adjust her trajectory.

But he also knew she wouldn't use the twins in her struggle against him, not even for a cause as vital as keeping him out of their lives. She'd never do anything to disturb them. So her threat didn't have any real power behind it.

Still, he couldn't let her suspect how anxious he was, how uncertain of his ability to conduct himself in any acceptable manner. For what constituted acceptable with eighteen-month-old toddlers? He knew far more about astrophysics and the latest trends in nail polish than about interacting with children. And it was almost beyond him to keep his upheaval in check.

But he had to pretend equanimity as he followed her

deeper into her exquisite home, the oasis of color, gaiety and contentment she'd built for her—for *their*—daughters, taking him to meet them for the first time. After he'd spent every day since they'd been born obsessing over their every detail.

Then she turned a corner into a great room equipped with a short plastic fence, decorative and sturdy, and just enough to keep little feet from wandering without detracting from the wide-open, welcoming feel of what must be every child's dream wonderland. And it was empty.

"Darling…"

Kassandra's breathy endearment made him stop. Suspended him in time.

She used to call him darling. Not always, just when she'd been incoherent with pleasure, which had been very frequently. The last time she'd said it to him he'd swiped at her proverbial jugular and severed it.

For heart-thudding moments, he didn't understand why she'd said it now, once, then again. Then he realized.

From what turned out to be an elaborate playhouse blended into the periphery of the room, a gleaming dark head peeked out of a tiny doorway, followed by an equally shiny golden one. She held out her arms and squeaks of glee issued from both girls as they competed to crawl out first, struggling to their feet as soon as they cleared the entrance. Two young cats, reflecting the girls' colorings, a black Angora and a golden Abyssinian, slinked out after them.

His heart contracted painfully. They were fast. He knew from his surveillance of them that their toddling had been improving every day. They were now almost running to their mother.

Kassandra went down on her haunches, preparing to receive them in her arms. But her descent only exposed him fully, bringing him into their line of vision. Their eyes rounded and their momentum slowed, both stopping just short of throwing themselves into her arms.

Knowing she was now no longer the focus of her girls' attention, Kassandra slowly stood up and slid him a sideways glance. Among the messages there was a challenge. He might have gotten what he'd demanded, but now she'd evaluate his performance and decide her consequent actions.

If he'd had any words left in him, he would have asked her to allow him a grace period without passing judgment. He'd fail her every test right now. Being face-to-face with those two tiny entities at last felt like a hurricane was uprooting everything inside him.

Before he could find his next breath, the twins rushed to stand behind Kassandra as she turned to him, each clinging to one endless jeans-clad leg and peeking up at him from the safety of their mother's barricade.

In contrast to their caution, the cats approached him, sniffing the air. Seeming to decide he didn't smell of danger, they neared him in degrees until they brushed against legs that felt as if they had grown roots. His throat tightened more as he bent without conscious thought to stroke them and receive head butts and arched backs. Then, seeming to consider this enough welcome for now, they sauntered away and jumped on shelves by the wall to watch the developing scene and groom themselves.

Unfolding with difficulty to his full height again, he found Kassandra with the miniatures of both of them staring at him. Avoiding her eyes, he focused on the girls'. Emerald eyes like Kassandra's and azure ones like his dominated faces that had occupied his thoughts since they'd been born. Two tiny sets of dewy rose lips rounded in questioning suspense.

"Vy oba...ideal'no."

It was only when chubby arms wrapped around their mother's legs tighter and those sparkling eyes widened more that he realized he'd spoken. Saying the one thing that filled his being. They were both perfect.

He waited. For Kassandra to say something. To introduce him. But she was silent, continuing to add the weight of her watchful gaze to theirs.

His mind crowded with everything he'd longed to do since they'd taken their first breaths. To swoop down and scoop them up in his arms was foremost among those urges.

But he knew there was no way this would be welcomed by Eva and Zoya, who were hanging on his every breath, bracing for his every move. They probably hadn't scurried back into their hiding place only because their mother was showing no signs of alarm, calmly facing him as if he was no threat, or at least one she was capable of protecting them from. It was as if they'd never seen anyone like him. Which was strange. He knew for a fact that their world was filled with big and imposing-looking men. The three men Kassandra had sent after him, and Kassandra's male relatives.

So why did he feel such total surprise emanating from them? Could it be they instinctively felt the bond between them?

Unable to decide, he emptied his mind, let his instincts take over. He trusted them now far more than he trusted his messed-up emotions and stalled logic.

He moved away from the trio training all their senses on him, circumventing them in a wide circle that took him to the playhouse the girls had exited. His aching gaze took in the evidence of their play session and of Kassandra's doting care. The strewn toys, coloring books and crayons, the half-built castle, the half-eaten finger foods and half-finished smoothies.

He'd missed all that. Everything, from their first day. He hadn't held them or comforted them or cleaned or served them or played with them or put them to bed. Kassandra had been alone in doing all that. Would any of them ever accept him into their lives, let him into their routines? Or even let him in any way at all? When he didn't deserve to be let in?

Feeling all eyes in the room on him, he went down on his knees, one of the hardest moves for him now. As he felt their surprise spike, he started to gather the toys and books.

Without looking back, so he'd give the girls respite from his focus, give them a sense of control and security, he started to order everything they'd knocked off onto the lushly carpeted floor on the low, sturdy plastic table. Out of the corner of his eyes, he saw Kassandra moving toward the long couch that dominated the opposite side of the space, with both girls still flocking around her legs, their gazes clinging to him.

Sampling one of the thin pineapple spears that were laid out on a cartoon-character tray among other healthy and colorful foods, he said, "That's very tasty. Can I have some more? I haven't eaten all day."

In his peripheral vision he could see the girls exchanging a glance, as if they understood his words and knew they were meant for them. Then they both looked up to their mother, as if seeking her permission to react. He stole a glance at her, found her giving them an exquisite smile. A special one he'd never seen, no doubt reserved only for them. Then she nodded, and they simultaneously let go of her legs and advanced toward him tentatively.

As they approached, he sat down on the ground, another challenging move, putting himself more at their level. This appeared to reassure them even more as their steps picked up speed. He pointed at a blunt skewer of cheese, cucumbers and strawberries, making direct eye contact with one girl, then the other. "Can I have that?"

The girls stopped on the other side of the table, eyes full of questions and curiosity. Then after what seemed to be serious consideration, Eva, the mini-Kassandra, reached out and grabbed the skewer in her dimpled hand...and leaned over to give it to him. Zoya, who'd held back, clearly more reserved like he was, took her cue from her older-by-ten-minutes sister, and repeated her action.

Throat closing, Leonid looked down on those two skewers, offered by the girls he'd fathered and hadn't been there for, until this moment. They were his life's biggest reward. And responsibility.

With hands that almost trembled out of control, he reached out and took both offerings at the same time. "That's very kind of you to share your snacks with me. *Spasiba*."

As if both recognized he'd just said a word in a language different from the one they'd been hearing and processing since birth, they looked at him questioningly.

"That is Russian. In English it means 'thank you.'" Then he repeated it a few times. "*Spasiba*...thank you."

Eyes gleaming at recognizing thank-you and clearly

making the connection between the two words, looking triumphant, Eva parroted him, "Patheba...thakyoo."

His heart thundered, its chambers just about melting
at Eva's adorable lisp.

And that was before Zoya delivered the second punch
of a one-two combo as she enthused, "Aseba...ankoo."

Before he could gather his wits, Eva picked up another skewer and proceeded to nibble at it, looking up
at him, as if encouraging him to eat. Zoya at once did
the same. When he didn't follow suit immediately, Zoya
reached out and pushed his hand up, urging him to par-
take of their offering.

He raised the food to lips that had gone numb, unable to taste anything as he chewed. Swallowing was an
even harder feat, pushing the food past the blockage in
his throat. All the time he could feel Kassandra's gaze
on him, scorching layers off his inflamed skin. It took
what was left of his control not to turn to her, ask for
her intervention.

But she didn't intervene. She didn't make a single
move, as if she was trying to blend into the background
to make them all forget she was there.

While that was what he'd asked her to do, now that he
had the girls' full attention and interest, he would have
given anything for her to dilute their focus. Which was
pathetic, since this was the opportunity he'd badgered
her for, what he'd been dreaming of for so long.

Inching closer now that they literally had him eating
out of their hands, the two girls started handing him their
favorite toys as more evidence of their acceptance, naming each one to show off their knowledge.

It became clear the second time they waited after
naming something that they were waiting for him to pro-

vide the Russian equivalent. And so it started, a game of translation.

The Russian word they loved the most was the one for *doll*. They both kept giggling and reiterating, *"Kukla... kukla!"*

They then moved on to testing him. One of them presented a coloring book and the other the crayons. When he colored a pony in a color scheme that was different from all the examples in the colored pages, they got more excited, and tried to emulate him in other books. After a while, dissatisfied with their own results compared to his impeccable ones, they reverted to the name-and-translate game.

Suddenly Eva seemed to realize she'd forgotten a vital issue. Then she pointed at herself and said, with a great sense of importance, "Eva."

Not to be outdone, Zoya immediately pointed to herself and said, "Zoya."

Then they both pointed at him, demanding he reciprocated the introduction.

He struggled to make his voice sound as normal as possible. "Leonid."

Not expecting them to be able to say such an abrupt name, they both surprised him by repeating accurately. "Leonid."

Swallowing past the growing pain in his throat, he felt the urge to complete the introduction, even when he knew they wouldn't understand the significance. *"Ya tvoy Papa.* This is also in Russian. It means 'I'm your father.'"

Feeling terminally stupid for speaking in such long sentences, and in two languages, too, when they at most only knew a few dozen words in English and maybe also in Greek, he smiled shakily, waiting for their attempt at the word.

This time they almost gave him a heart attack.

Getting to the heart of what he'd said, they both pointed at him and chorused, "Papa."

By now, Kassandra had gotten used to her heart's erratic function. Since Leonid had appeared on her doorstep, it had been stopping periodically before it stampeded out of control in compensation.

From the moment the girls hadn't run to welcome him as they did anyone who entered their home with her, she'd known.

They'd at once realized he wasn't just a friend or an acquaintance, but someone on a totally different level from anyone they'd seen before. Far more important than even Kassandra's family. Someone on par in importance to them with Kassandra herself.

Kassandra had bated her breath, dreading that Leonid would botch this, knowing from their instant recognition of his significance to them that it would hurt them. But Leonid had proceeded to provide one shock after another, everything he'd done and said sensitive and inventive. He'd followed no known path with the girls, and soon had them so engrossed in his presence, they'd forgotten to include her.

What had at first rattled her with chagrin and jealousy had gradually become incredibly emotional, as she watched something she'd always dreamed of but never believed would come to pass. The girls with their father, the only other person who should love them as completely as she did, behaving as if they'd known him all their lives. She couldn't have interacted with the trio had they asked.

Hours could have passed since they'd become immersed in one another. She'd lost track of self and time as she'd watched them. She'd even lost sight of her memories of the past and everything that had led to this situation. All she could see was her girls delighting in their father, and him appearing to delight in them back.

And then came their fervent proclamation that he was their "papa." Just as her stalled heart sputtered into a forced restart, Leonid stopped it again, saying so deeply and gently, "Yes, you brilliant girls, I'm your papa."

Before she could draw a breath, before she passed out and spoiled everything, the girls threw themselves at Leonid.

A surprised laugh issued from him as he hugged tight the small, robust bodies of her daughters. Kassandra reeled, trying to make sense of this.

She could only think the girls had always realized other kids had papas while they didn't. Then they had seen Leonid and simply recognized him as their own papa. Once they'd approved him through their own brand of testing, and he'd validated their belief, they'd accepted him in their own unique way.

No, they'd more than accepted him. They'd claimed him.

It was funny she'd think of this specific term, what he'd already used about them. But nothing else described what was happening in front of her eyes. It was a claiming. Declared and accepted, on both sides.

Leonid, who'd been doing everything right to put the girls at ease, from body language to expression to tone of voice, now rumbled with unfettered laughter as the girls

attacked him with their zeal. But what he did next had
her slumping back against the couch in a nerveless mass.

He sprawled flat on the ground, letting the girls prowl
all over his great body. Thrilled by his action and the
invitation it afforded them, they drowned him in hugs
and kisses before launching into examining every inch
of his very-different-to-hers body and clothes, acquaint-
ing themselves with the details of that new powerful entity they'd made their own.

Then she started to worry again. That this would still
end badly, that Leonid would be appalled or fed up by
their level of enthusiasm and attention. Would he decide
he'd made a mistake coming near them and withdraw?
Then she scolded herself for worrying. She should hope
for that to happen so he'd leave, let them return to their
contented status quo. As for the girls' psyches, they were
young enough that if he disappeared now, no matter his
impact on them, they'd soon forget him.

Just as she'd come to this conclusion and was pulling herself up to intervene, he looked up at her from his
flat-on-his-back position on the floor, covered in toddler limbs and laughter, with a grin she'd never seen on
his face before.

"Any help here?"

Okay, that didn't look like the face or attitude of a man
who was regretting anything. His call for help seemed to
be part of the game, maybe his way of including her in it.

Forcing her feet to function, she approached the
merry mass on the ground made up of the beings who
mattered most to her. Leonid once, and her girls forever.

She stopped over them, her lips quirking involuntarily
at the infectious gaiety at her feet.

"What help does the unstoppable future king require?"

Eyes that had haunted her for the past five years flashed azure merriment up at her, the stiff stranger of the first two encounters gone. "I have no idea. But I can tell you that if you don't do something and they don't let me up, you may have to let me spend the night right here on the ground."

"Take heart. In a worst-case scenario, they'll keep you there until they fall asleep. Once they do, I can get them off you and you'll be free to get up."

Eva pulled his face toward her to show him another toy, a miniature lion. After he told her it was *lev* and she dutifully repeated her own version of the word, Zoya pointed to her cat Shadow, who'd come to join the fun with Goldie. After he told her both the word for *cat* and their breeds in Russian and she did the same, he swung his gaze back to Kassandra.

"Do they usually use you as a mattress or am I getting special treatment?"

"You're the one who made yourself one. But then, I'm nowhere as big and comfortable as you are."

She knew that from extensive experience. Going to sleep spread over him after long, depleting nights of excruciating pleasure.

Thankfully, he wasn't the man he'd been. That man would have latched on to that comment, teasing and provoking her. That man had been raging wildfire, while this new man was a bottomless ocean. His unexpected behavior with the girls was just another depth to him she hadn't thought could exist.

He broke eye contact when the quartet of girls and cats demanded his attention. Then one duo was climbing off him only for the other to climb on. With only the cats to contend with, he sat up, with them roaming his lap. Eva and Zoya called him to another part of their playroom, and he looked at her again, seeming to find some trouble rising to his feet.

Her heart gave a sick lurch. It appeared his injuries had never fully healed, as she'd once feared. He hid it well, but now that she was looking for evidence of it, she could see his gait wasn't normal. After sitting on the floor for so long, it was harder for him to conceal.

Not that she was about to feel bad for him. He'd never needed or even tolerated her empathy. The best she could be was civil, and it was only for the girls' sake.

After he followed the girls to their sandbox in the adjoining enclosed terrace, he looked back at her.

"So you enlisted The Savage Sarantoses and the Big Bad Russian Wolf's help to…deal with me."

Not knowing what to make of his attitude, if he was angry about her siccing them on him, or taunting her about her effort's failure, she arched an eyebrow. "Should've saved my breath. They turned out to be neither savage nor big and bad. You neutralized them as if by magic."

His lips twitched as he kneeled where the girls indicated at the edge of their sandbox, clearly unconcerned by the damages his handmade suit would certainly suffer.

With a shovel in hand, he slanted her another glance that set her insides quivering. "No spells were involved. But I applaud your effort. It was a very sound strategy. That it didn't work doesn't make it any less so."

Was he…entertained by her struggle against him? Teasing her about its futility? If he was, it was a more understated form of provocation than anything he'd ever exposed her to. And whether she was more susceptible now, or he was more potent, it was far more...unsettling.

"Join me in building a castle for our princesses?"

For several long seconds she could only stare at him. It had just dawned on her.

Eva and Zoya were actual princesses.

When one daunting eyebrow prodded a response from her, she made herself move. She came down on her knees far enough from him to keep her agitation at manageable levels, but close enough to work with him, if need be. The girls flitted between them, handing them tools, then climbing inside to make their own little molds as she and Leonid started collaborating on something intricate.

Trying to focus on what they were doing, she said, "I've never attempted anything elaborate, since their appreciation takes the form of destructive admiration. Then they're crestfallen when my creations crumble."

He shrugged those endless shoulders. "I'll try to make them realize how to preserve it, but if they level it or it's time to replace it, I'll make them understand I'll build them another. In time, I'll teach them how to build their own."

"You seem certain you can get all this across."

"I am. They're extremely intelligent and very receptive."

She almost blurted out that while they were indeed intelligent, she'd only seen this level of receptiveness directed at him. But she held her tongue. The admission would only complicate matters further.

From then on, there were stretches of silence between them as they worked, with Leonid taking the lead, creating a castle that looked like a miniature of a real one in every detail. Then, true to his conviction, he curbed the girls' appetite for destruction, encouraging them to expend their excitement in making flower and animal molds to surround it.

Then it was time for the girls' dinner, and he pounced on the chance to feed them, insisting on handling the soup part. He managed to complete the task with even less mess than she usually did. And he'd turned the whole thing into another game, pointing to kitchen articles with each spoonful, getting names in English, correcting and translating what the girls didn't know. The girls competed to provide answers, and get Papa's attention and appreciation.

An hour after dinner, two hours after their bedtime, the girls lost the fight to prolong their wakefulness to remain with Leonid. And they again did something unprecedented. Instead of turning to her, they went to him, arms raised, demanding to be picked up. At once complying, he gathered them in a secure hold, where they both promptly dozed off.

Without a word, she led him to the nursery, where he placed them, one after the other, in their cribs. She stood with bated breath, waiting to see what he'd do next as he remained standing over them, his eyes wells of mystery in the dimness.

At length, he bent and kissed them. Each girl gave a contented gurgle at his tender caress before assuming her favorite sleeping position.

Straightening, he led the way out of the room, then headed straight for the door. He didn't look her way until he'd opened it and stepped outside.

"Thank you for tonight."

With that, he turned and slowly walked down the steps. In a minute, he climbed into his car and drove away.

Closing the door, she automatically armed her security system, turned off the lights and headed to her room.

It was only after she'd gone through her nighttime routine and slipped into bed that she let it all crash on her. Everything he'd said and done all through the evening, everything about him.

Nothing made sense anymore.

For two years, the last thing she'd wanted was Leonid near again. Now, she was forced to face the truth.

She'd wanted him to come near tonight. So much that his pointed avoidance of her had felt like a knife in her gut. It still twisted there now.

She might have been able to handle it if she'd had any hope he would stay away from her altogether. But after this incredible first meeting between him and her...his... *their* daughters, she knew there was no hope for that.

Leonid would be in their lives. If everything she'd felt from him toward the girls tonight was real, and she couldn't doubt it was, she could no longer deny him, or them, that reality.

Which meant he would be in her life, too, maybe even forever.

The only man she'd ever wanted.

When he'd long stopped wanting her.

Four

A rewind button had yanked Kassandra back into her worst days—only with an even darker twist. For this time, it wasn't Leonid discarding her, leaving her desolate and then disappearing. He was now planning to stay around forever.

After she'd thought she'd been cured of any emotions she'd felt for him, she'd woken up today with her resolve to stay neutral pulverized. It had taken him exactly four hours last night to show her how self-deluding she'd been, how susceptible to his magic she remained. How pathetic she was.

If only he'd lived up to her expectations, had been the unfeeling entity he'd been with her, with the girls. It would have given her ammunition to stop him coming near them again. It would have saved her from stumbling back into the abyss of longing. But he'd been…perfect.

Worse, they'd *all* been perfect together. It had been like she'd watched scattered pieces of a vital whole finally clicking together. She of all people recognized and realized the significance of what she'd witnessed. Her very self had been built around a tight relationship with her father as much as her mother. She knew exactly how wonderful such a relationship could be, how essential a loving paternal influence was. And just by being wonderful with the girls, he'd snatched away her last weapon against him, that of his potential disruptiveness to the girls' psyches and lives. Now she had to let him be the girls' father, as she could no longer doubt he truly wanted to be. She had to let the girls have him as the other half of their world, while trying to preserve her sanity with him around. But now that she'd discovered her unilateral fixation with him had never weakened, she had no idea how she'd achieve that.

Dwelling on that terrible fate had to be postponed. Now she had work to do, far more than usual since she hadn't worked a lick since he'd reappeared. The summer line wouldn't approve itself and put itself into production.

Walking into her design house's new headquarters, she concentrated on being attentive and friendly with each and every one of her employees. She'd done it wholeheartedly so many times she could do it on autopilot now.

Reaching her office, she thought she'd escaped with her turmoil undetected, anxious to plunge into work, the only thing that would ameliorate it. But the moment she entered, she knew salvaging her schedule would have to wait. Right there in her sitting area were three of the people her staff knew to let into her private space without question.

Her best friends.

It should have been a shock to find them here, as dropping by her office on a whim was no longer something they did with her on the other side of the continent. It should have at least been a surprise. It was neither. Seemed Leonid had depleted her reserves for shock and surprise for the foreseeable future.

Bracing herself for what she knew would come, she plastered a smile back onto her face.

Selene was the first to rise to her feet, despite being the most heavily pregnant of them all. Yes, they were all pregnant. Again. Selene and Caliope were now on their third babies. Naomi, too, even if it was only her second biological one, with her first child being her late sister's.

After kissing and hugging her, Caliope and Naomi let Selene, as her oldest friend, lead the interrogation.

Selene shot her opening salvo, getting to the point at once. "What exactly is going on with Leonid?"

Kassandra's lips twisted. "You tell me. Your husbands are the ones who have answers."

Something that resembled annoyance tinged Selene's deep blue eyes. "They haven't been forthcoming, for the first time since the days they were closed-off icebergs. Each aggravating man only said it's for the best that you and Leonid work this out alone."

Kassandra flopped down on an armchair across from the couch where they sat facing her like a tribunal. "And you clearly disagree and that's why you're here."

"You scared the hell out of us when you called!" Caliope exclaimed. "We've never heard you so distressed. And when it comes to you, even our men's words aren't enough."

Naomi nodded, looking as concerned. "We had to get the final word from the source."

Kassandra huffed a mirthless chuckle. "And that's me?"

Selene's gaze softened and hardened at once. "You don't call for the big guns—who clearly didn't fire a shot—then answer our messages with more vagueness, and expect us to sit back and wait."

Kassandra squeezed her friend's hand fondly. "Vagueness is an achievement in my situation, since I'm as in the dark as any of you. Your men left this office promising me they'd leash Leonid away from me and the girls. Then each called me to cajole me into giving him a full and fair chance."

"A chance at what exactly?" Caliope sat forward, reaching for Kassandra's other hand, her smooth brow furrowing. "This is the part no one is clear on."

"At being the girls' father."

"Is that all he wants a chance at?" Naomi probed.

"Yes."

"You mean he didn't…?"

"Didn't ask for a second chance with me? No. According to him, he never wanted a first one."

"He said that?" Selene's gaze hardened to granite.

Knowing she was sealing Leonid's coffin where her friends were concerned, Kassandra sighed. "What amounted to that. When he was breaking it off, he made it clear he considered our liaison only sexual entertainment and he'd had enough long before he told me to get the hell away from him when I failed to take a hint."

Caliope, the softest heart among them, piped up. "He was at his worst when he said that. It could have been his frustration and anger at the whole world talking."

Exactly what Kassandra had thought at first. She

shrugged. "He disappeared for over two years. Too long to be at your worst."

"Maybe he realized the gravity of his mistake," Naomi offered, her newest bestie, the one clearly trying to keep emotions out of the equation. "But didn't know how to fix it."

"You mean he stayed away because he couldn't face me?" Kassandra huffed. "This is a man who has faced tens of thousands of people on the athletic field, the rest of the world when he was in the rabid spotlight of the media, not to mention the sharks of business he wrestled under the table on a regular basis. He squared off with *your* unstoppable predators and turned them into purring pussycats."

Selene exhaled heavily. "This last bit *is* something we're all beyond perplexed about. We thought only us and the kids could do this to our Triumvirate."

Kassandra gave a there-you-go gesture. "Since you know your endless power over your men, you can measure Leonid's."

Caliope's eyes shone. "Maybe *that's* your answer, since when it comes to us, our men's rules are inverted. Maybe it's the same with Leonid. The man who can make the world heel could be powerless when it comes to you."

That was the last straw. She had to put a stop to her friends' efforts to give her hope that her story could end as happily as theirs.

Sitting forward, she let any lightness she'd painted on drain from her face. "Okay, let me make one thing clear. My situation with Leonid is nothing like yours with your men. Those men were more than ninety percent in love with you when each left you or let you go or did whatever they did. Leonid never felt a thing for me, and he'd been itching to move on. He would have done so without the accident, but it gave him the opportunity to do it abruptly." And viciously. She'd never been able to bring herself to tell them just how viciously. "Now he's only back for the girls. He made this far more than clear."

Echoes of her hard tone and words rang in the silence that stretched afterward. A myriad of emotions streaked across the women's faces, each according to her character and relationship with Kassandra. What they shared seemed to be mortification, empathy…and fury.

Selene was first to gather her wits enough to ask another question. "Are you even considering giving him that chance?"

"Since I don't have a way of keeping him away, and since my reasons for wanting to do so no longer apply, I don't have the choice not to."

"So you're feeling forced into it." Naomi chewed her lip thoughtfully. "Would you have considered his return and his demand more favorably if he was back for you, too?"

"No." Kassandra paused, then had to add, "Not at first."

And *that* told them everything. That after everything he'd put her through, she still wanted him. That after her initial anger and rejection, her buried emotions had resurfaced, and she now wished he wanted her, too. Which he didn't.

Clearly realizing all that, anger set Selene's exquisite features on fire. "I don't care how he got Aris and the others on his side, I'll make them wipe him off the face of the earth. And if they don't, we three can still do a lot of damage on our own."

Caliope nodded. "You know we would do anything for you."

"Even if it means standing against your husbands?"

The three women's exclamations were simultaneous.

"Just say the word."

"Without hesitation."

"Hell, yeah."

Kassandra's eyes stung, a smile shaking her lips. "And I love you, too. But that won't be necessary. Everything changed, literally overnight. He came to visit the girls last night. And no matter what I feel, how he was with them, how they were with him, makes him deserve that full and fair chance he's convinced your men he should get."

"That man crushed your heart," Selene ground out. "And I have a feeling if he invades your life again to be with the girls, he'll hurt you again."

Kassandra sighed. "And I can't do anything about it. It's not his or the girls' fault he feels nothing for me."

Caliope threw her hands up in the air. "You should have moved on when you got the chance. *All* those chances. There were at least three men who could have been perfect for you! And they're all still waiting for your slightest signal."

"Could any of you have moved on when you were estranged from your own member of the Triumvirate?" The three women winced, lips twisting in concession. "Exactly. Same here."

"But if you know nothing would come out of it because you're feeling this way about the wrong man..."

"The problem is he isn't the wrong man," Kassandra said, interrupting Naomi. "Apart from his treatment of me and his lack of feelings for me, he remains everything I admire in a man. And though I hate it and wish it wasn't so, the fact remains that no one withstands the comparison to him in my eyes."

"But you can't just resign yourself to being miserable like this!" Selene exclaimed, her face reddening.

"As long as Eva and Zoya are happy, it's a price I have to pay. You would pay the same price and more for your kids."

"How do you know he'll make them happy?" Selene countered.

"Surely you can't tell from one meeting!" Calliope added.

Kassandra sighed. "Regretfully for me, and fortunately for them, I can. You have to see them together to understand."

Selene wouldn't give up that easily. "What if, once the novelty wears off, he becomes the son of a bitch he was with you with them?"

Kassandra set her teeth. "If he even breathes wrong around them, I'll rip out his jugular."

"That's our Kassandra!" Selene's approval was ferocious.

Caliope's face fell. "So the only thing that can make you hate him is if there's a hint of mistreatment or neglect toward Eva and Zoya. Which you don't seem to think would happen."

Naomi was as crestfallen. "*And* we can't even wish it."

"Can't we?" Selene growled protectively. "They wouldn't lose anything if he exited their lives as he entered it. They were perfectly fine without him after all."

"They were." Kassandra exhaled heavily. "But with him in their lives, they could be far more than fine. You really have to—"

"See them together to understand?" Caliope sighed. "Not really. If his effect on the girls is anything like Maksim's effect on our children, I know exactly what you're talking about."

Selene looked more horrified by the second. "So you're stuck with him? You have to suffer forever and we have to watch it and be unable to do anything about it?"

Wanting to alleviate her friend's distress on her behalf and end this debate once and for all, Kassandra decided to placate them. "Who knows? Maybe I'm just experiencing echoes of what I once felt for him, and being around him again will show me I've blown everything out of proportion, allowing me to move on at last. Maybe this will turn out to be a blessing in disguise after all."

The three women looked at her, then exchanged a look among themselves before finally nodding. It was evident they hoped so with all their hearts. But even though they let her change the subject, she knew they didn't believe this was even in the realm of possibility.

Not for a second.

At last, Selene rose to her feet, prompting the others to do so, too. As Kassandra followed suit, Selene waddled toward her, holding out both hands to pull her into a tight hug. At least as tight as her burgeoning belly allowed.

Drawing back, Selene's dark blue eyes were almost grim. "If you change your mind and you need help getting rid of him, I'll do anything."

"Ditto," the other two chorused.

Choking on a cry, Kassandra surged to envelop them in a group hug, thanking the fates for them.

Pulling back, she gave her friends a wobbly smile. "Next time I know who to run to when I need impenetrable barriers against unstoppable missiles. What was I thinking asking for your men's help when I have you?"

Selene's features relaxed into a mischievous smile. "As long as you've learned your mistake. Right, ladies?"

Caliope and Naomi expressed their enthusiastic agreement, and the meeting that had started out tense ended on a merry note.

As merry as a breather in the ongoing drama that had become her life could be.

After her friends left her office, Kassandra struggled to get any work done. But as all the lightheartedness and optimism their love and support had brought her started to dissipate, she was dragged back into the bottomless well of worries and what-ifs.

Though she'd planned to stay at work hours longer, and she'd only done a fraction of what she'd set out to do, she gave up. At least at home she wouldn't have to make decisions that had millions of dollars and hundreds of jobs riding on them. Decisions she was starting to doubt she'd be able to make again.

Half an hour later, as she entered her home, a shroud of premonition descended around her heart. Though there was no car parked outside, and there were no sounds coming from inside, all her senses rioted with certainty.

Leonid was in there. She could scent him in the air, sense his presence in her every cell.

Trying to curb her stampeding reactions, she leaned on the wall, only to feel it tilt beneath her. Struggling with the wave of dizziness, she shrugged out of her suddenly suffocating coat, was trying to hang it when Kyria

Despina came rushing toward her, her expression the very definition of awe.

"Kassandra, dearest, I'm so glad you're home early!" The woman's voice buzzed with excitement as she took Kassandra's coat and hung it in the foyer's closet. "Prince Voronov has been here for two hours."

So he was here. Seemed her extrasensory abilities where he was concerned remained infallible.

Dark brown eyes gleaming with curiosity and pleasure, Despina linked their arms as she hurried Kassandra to the living room. "He came thinking you'd be back home at your usual time. The girls were beside themselves with delight to see him."

Feeling her legs about to buckle as the quietly prattling Despina led her to him, her mind was a battlefield of suspense, aversion and resignation. Confusion soon took precedence over the absolute silence emanating from the living room.

Then they reached it and it all made sense.

At the end of the room, Leonid was propped up against the playhouse. The girls were asleep on top of him. The cats were also snoozing, one on his legs, the other against his thigh.

"He played with them nonstop, games I'm sure he invented just for them," Despina whispered. "The darlings laughed and bounced around like I've never seen them. Then about fifteen minutes before you arrived, they climbed on his lap and turned off. The dear man made them comfortable, even crooned what must be a Russian nursery rhyme."

They'd slept on top of him. They hadn't fallen asleep in her arms since they were six months old.

"He hasn't moved or made a sound since, even when

I assured him nothing would wake them up again. You should go save him before he cramps something." Despina patted her on the back. "Now, since you're home and he's here to help you put the girls to bed, I may yet catch a bit of the ladies' poker night I had to miss to stay late tonight."

As if from the depths of a dream, Kassandra thought she nodded her agreement. Then everything fell off her radar but the sight Leonid and the girls made, a majestic lion with his cubs curled in slumber over him, totally content and secure in their father's presence and protection.

His eyes remained closed, but she knew he wasn't asleep. She could sense it. He was savoring the texture of the new experience, soaking in the girls' feel and closeness and trust. She also knew he was aware of her standing there. Like her, he'd always had an uncanny ability to sense her presence. She'd once thought he'd been so attuned to her, he felt her before he had reason to think she was near. That had been before she'd realized she'd never been special or even worthwhile to him.

Swallowing the lump that seemed to have taken permanent residence in her throat, she approached the pile. He let her come within less than a foot of them before he opened his eyes, connecting with hers, and almost compromised her precarious balance. Then he lowered his gaze to the girls in his arms again.

Forcing air into her shut-down lungs, she attempted nonchalance. "You can flip the girls in the air and they still wouldn't wake. Not now anyway. They only wake up around an hour after I put them in bed."

"Did they wake up last night after I left?"

"No."

She'd told herself they hadn't because he'd kept them way beyond their bedtime. But apart from logic, another theory explained the unusual occurrence. She believed that they always woke up out of some sense of uncertainty. But after he'd appeared, and they'd sensed his intention of being here to stay, that anxiety that woke them up was gone.

She exhaled. "My point is, you can move if you want."

"I don't want. There's no place I'd rather be."

What felt like acid welled behind her eyes. "Well, though you do look as if you make them very comfortable, I don't think they should start considering you a substitute for their bed."

His lips twisted as he kept gazing at the shiny heads nestled into his chest. "Though I would fully welcome that, I can appreciate the repercussions of such a development."

Sighing as he secured them both, he sat up. She again almost winced at the difficulty he had in adjusting his position, of rising to his feet. It had nothing to do with the girls being in his arms, since their weight had to be negligible to him. That knot behind her sternum, the same one that had formed when she'd realized the extent of his injuries and their consequences, tightened to an ache again.

Taking her eyes off him, so she wouldn't focus on his stiff gait and the fact that he was looking everywhere but at her, she led the way to the nursery, her mind racing.

Though the competition circuits were certainly out, had it been possible for him to practice his sports on any level? Being extremely fit but bulkier than before, it was clear he maintained his fitness with exercise that didn't rely on the speed and agility of his former specialties. So how much did he resent being forced to relinquish what he'd considered the epitome of his personal achievement? How much did he miss what had once been the main pillar of his existence?

Giving herself the mental equivalent of a smack upside the head as they put the girls in the cribs, she reminded herself how pointless and pathetic it was to wonder. Whatever his trials to adjust his path, and whatever he'd suffered or now felt about it all was none of her concern. He'd made that clear in the past. He was making it clearer now. This was all about Eva and Zoya. Beyond what she represented to them, she, and anything she thought and felt, mattered nothing to him.

As they exited the room, he finally looked at her. "I hope it's not your habit to sleep as soon as they do. I have a few things I need to discuss with you."

She stifled the urge to hiss that she'd lost the habit of sleeping altogether since him, that she had to exhaust herself on a daily basis only so she could turn off and hope for the oppressive silence and darkness of dreamlessness.

Managing to reach her living room without blasting his thick hide off, she sat down carefully instead of flinging herself on the couch. She also refrained from hurling a remote at him as he remained towering over her.

"How would you like to go about declaring me the girls' father?"

Blinking, her mind emptied. Had she heard him right? He wasn't dictating a course of action, but asking her preference?

Suddenly her blood tumbled in a boil. "How about you spare me the pretense that you care about what I want?"

"I do care. As Eva's and Zoya's mother you are—"

"Entitled to dictate my own terms. Yeah, I heard it the first time. And I already told you, my only term is to have the life I built for myself and the girls. But since this isn't going to happen, just do what you wish, and don't bother pretending that my preferences matter."

Those winged eyebrows she'd once luxuriated in tracing with fingertips and lips knotted as he seemed to examine every fiber in her lush carpet. The way he kept avoiding making eye contact with her at crucial moments was driving her up the wall.

He finally exhaled, his gaze once again on her and maddening her with its opacity. "That first night I came, I had to drive it home that I wasn't taking *go away* for an answer. But ever since I met the twins, and we interacted as their parents, many things have changed. I do want this arrangement to work for you, not only for them."

She never thought he'd say those words—and he actually seemed to mean them. It made everything even worse. Anger was her only defense against him, her last shield. If he made her let that go, what would become of her?

But that was a consideration for another time. For the rest of her lifetime. Now she had to give him an answer.

The truth was the only thing she had. "I haven't given any thought to how I'll break the news about you being the girls' father. I suppose I'll just tell the people I care about. Anyone else doesn't matter. Even if I am a public figure, I'm not in the spotlight nearly as much as you and my importance to the media is nothing compared to yours. You're also the one with a kingdom to consider in your public statements from now on. I'll leave it up to you to announce this as you see fit."

"In that case, I'll move on to the major reason I came." Suddenly, she wished she hadn't resented his lack of eye contact as his gaze transfixed hers, paralyzing her with a bolt of blue lightning. And that was before he said, "I came to ask you to marry me."

Five

"Marry you?"

Kassandra wasn't even sure she'd said that out loud. From the way her voice sounded, as if issuing from beneath a ton of rubble, maybe it was in her head. All of it. Including what he'd just said, so earnestly, asking her to...

"*Marry* you?"

This time she was sure she'd said it, judging by the urgency that surged in his eyes.

"I'm only asking this for Eva and Zoya."

Of course. None of it was or had ever been for her.

"It's the only way to secure their legitimacy."

"Legitimacy..." She parroted him again, her shock deepening.

She hadn't even thought of this aspect of things before. But he had said he'd *claim* them, and she'd vaguely realized he meant giving them his name. Yet the significance of that, that it would make them "legitimate," had escaped her. Now, knowing the implications, it felt so…offensive.

Fury flooded her, drowning her shock. "Legitimacy is an outdated concept. My daughters aren't and won't ever be defined or even affected by it. In this day and age, it's not a stigma anymore to have children out of wedlock." Suddenly, the room spun, making her slouch back on the couch. "And will you quit looming over me like this?"

He sat down at once, still careful to keep her at arm's length. His eyes took on a hypnotic edge, as if trying to compel her to succumb to his demand.

"Legitimacy wouldn't have mattered to me if I was anyone else. I would have become their father in all ways that matter and left it up to you when or if you let them have my name on official papers. But as you just pointed out, with my future role, bowing to the social and political mores of my kingdom has become imperative. Eva and Zoya aren't only my daughters, they're my heirs. They have to carry my name."

"And marrying me is the only way to have them carry your name instead of mine?"

"Not instead, with yours. I want them to have both our family names. They would be Eva and Zoya Stavros Voronov."

Her heart kicked her ribs so hard she almost keeled over. Those names. They sounded so…right.

But still… "We can do that without getting—"

He shook his majestic head, cutting her off.

"Getting married is also an unquestionable necessity. Consider that not even in recent history has the president of a progressive country had children out of wedlock. It isn't even a possibility for a king in Zorya. Our marriage isn't only a must for social acceptance and political stability in this case, it's also the only guarantee of the twins' rights and privileges as my heirs."

"*And* the restrictions and responsibilities, maybe even dangers. Even if you prove to be a great father to them, and that would be in their best interests, being heirs to the precarious throne of such a stuck-in-time kingdom isn't."

The azure of his eyes darkened to cobalt. "While your worries are logical, I pledge I will protect them from anything in this world, starting with any drawbacks of their title and my position. It's part of the reason why I'm taking the crown in Zorya. To see to it that it retains its useful traditions, but discards any backward practices. It must fully join the modern world where it matters on every level, be it social or political or economical. I will make Zorya a land I would be proud to raise our daughters in."

His fervent convictions and assured intentions seeped into her thoughts, suppressing misgivings and painting an enchanted future she'd certainly want for Eva and Zoya. Then his last words sank in with a thud, jogging her out of the trance.

"You mean you expect us to move there?"

"It's the only way for me to be in the twins' lives constantly, but it's you who'll dictate how to divide your time between Zorya and the United States. Of course, it would be ideal if you move to Zorya now."

She gaped at him, feeling as if she was watching a movie playing so fast everything had ceased to make sense.

"If you fear being in Zorya would interrupt the normal flow of your life, don't. I'll have every resource constantly at your disposal. You'll be able to travel anywhere in the world at a moment's notice. And when you have to be somewhere for any length of time, or even return here for an extended period, of course the girls will be with you, and I'll arrange my affairs so that I may join you as much as possible."

His assurances again underlined the extent of his power and wealth. But only one thing kept screeching like a siren in her mind.

"You expect me—us—to live with you in Zorya, and when we're back here...?"

His hand rose in a placating gesture. "You'll have your own quarters in the royal palace with the twins. I will visit them there according to the schedule you set, or have them with me within the parameters you approve. When you return here for visits or for longer stretches and I join you, I will arrange my own accommodations. I'm ready to provide all of these terms and any others you specify in a legally binding format."

This nightmare was getting darker with his every word. Though he was insisting she'd retain control of all decisions that shaped the girls' daily lives and futures, his every promise made her more heartsick. It all reinforced the simple fact that they were adversaries forced to come to an understanding. He'd progressed from bulldozing her to drawing legal lines to protect her share of rights, and no doubt his own. The only interactions they would have would be with the girls and through them, with them playing the part of polite partners in their presence and in front of others. Or would he ask her to play the part of a loving bride in front of the latter...?

Then he answered her uncertainties. "You have nothing to worry about when it comes to my presence in your life. In front of the girls, you need only keep doing what you have. In front of others, it's accepted for royal couples to be reserved in public, so you don't need to worry about putting on a facade of intimacy. In both private and public, our relationship would remain as it is."

In other words, nonexistent.

"I expect you'll have your own demands and modifications and I intend to fully accommodate your every wish."

Feeling the quicksand dragging her down into its depths even harder, she choked out, "You're talking as if I've already accepted, as if the only thing to do now is vet out details."

He stilled. "Why wouldn't you accept?"

"Why?" She huffed in incredulity. "Are you for real? This is my *life* you're turning upside down."

"I gave you my pledge your life won't be affected in any adverse way, but only enhanced. You'd be a queen…"

The word *queen* went off like a gong inside her head.

She found herself on her feet, staring down at him, shaking from head to toe. "You think I care about that title or could even want it? I never wanted *anything* but to raise my daughters in privacy and peace, and with you in our lives, there will never be either of those things ever again!"

He rose slowly to his feet, and even in her distress her muscles contracted in empathy at the difficulty he found in rising from her too-low couch. As he straightened, his balance wavered, and for seconds, he came so close, heat flaring from his body, in his eyes, and she thought he'd reach for her…touch her. All her nerves tangled, firing in unison.

Then he regained his stability and stepped back, leaving a cold draft in his wake. The blaze in his eyes was gone, as if she'd imagined it. Perhaps she had.

Turning, he walked to the opposite armchair, picked up the coat he'd draped over its back and put it on in measured movements. Then he came back to her where she stood ramrod tense.

He stopped even farther away than usual, his expression as impassive as ever. "I know this is too much to take in, so I'll leave you to think. I didn't expect you to give me an answer right away."

Trying to suppress her tremors, she failed to stem the shaking in her voice. "Are you even expecting any answer but yes? Would you accept any other answer?"

The perfect mask that had replaced his previously animated face became even harder to read. "Any other answer would be no. So no, I can't accept that."

Her lips twisted in bitterness. "So why are you pretending you'd give me time to think? Think of what? How to say yes? Or to reach the conclusion that it's pointless to say anything at all from now on, since you'll always do what you want anyway, using the girls' and your kingdom's best interests to silence my protests and misgivings and make me fall in line with your plans?"

His eyes dimmed even more. And she realized.

What she'd thought was meticulous impassiveness was something else altogether. Bleakness.

This epiphany silenced the rest of the tirade that had been brewing inside her. His despondency dug into her chest, snatching at her heart.

Was he distraught because he had to tie himself to

her? Was he feeling as hopeless as she was, sacrificing his freedom and what remained of his ambitions of pursuing what fulfilled *him*, for the girls' and his kingdom's sakes? Would being near her, to have access to his daughters, be too harsh a sentence to bear?

When she couldn't say anything more, he exhaled. "I didn't expect you'd welcome my proposition, but I do want you to take some time to think. Contrary to what you believe, there's a lot to consider, practical details that you need to sort out, questions you need to ask, demands you will want to make. I regret this is unavoidable but I pledge I will comply with any measures you specify to make everything as painless as possible."

As painless as possible.

The words ricocheted in Kassandra's head until she felt they'd pulped her brain.

He didn't even realize he'd already done the most painful thing he could have. Proposing marriage, for everyone's and everything's sake but hers.

What made it all worse was admitting she would have jumped at his proposal if there'd been any hope they could have rekindled a fraction of what they'd once had. His offer would have even been somewhat acceptable, for all other considerations, if he wasn't as averse to her being a constant part of his life.

But with both of them feeling they'd be imprisoned for life, there was no way she could accept.

Forcing her focus back on him, now that she saw through his expressionlessness, it battered her heart to feel the gloom gripping his stance, the dejection that blasted from him.

She struggled not to sound as shredded as she felt. "Even if I believe you'd keep every word, and though I understand the need for this step, I *can't* say yes. But I have an alternative. We can tell everyone we are already married but estranged, and that we decided to get back together. I would play my part for as long as you need to 'claim' the girls to fulfill your kingdom's traditional requirements, solving all your problems without creating a bigger one…for both of us."

His gaze dropped to the ground he now seemed to find so fascinating. Then without even a nod, he turned away.

Feeling him recede, she stared into nothingness, struggling to stem the bottled-up misery he'd stirred up.

The moment she heard him closing the front door with the softest thud, she broke down, let the storm overtake her.

Each time he'd gone to Kassandra, Leonid had sent away his driver and bodyguards.

The latter, fellow patriotic Zoryans who'd volunteered for the job and considered guarding him a sacred duty and ultimate honor, had always objected. There was no doubt in their minds anymore he'd become king, and his safety was no longer his personal concern, but a matter of national security and what the future of their kingdom rested on.

He'd still been adamant. He hadn't wanted anyone to know about Kassandra and the girls until he'd resolved everything with her. As he'd gone to her tonight bent on doing.

He'd parked miles away. He still found it hard to walk, always ended up in varying levels of discomfort after being on his feet and moving for a considerable length of time. And that was exactly what he'd needed tonight.

He'd needed the pain of exertion to dissipate some of the storm frying his system, the bite of cold to chill a measure of the inferno that had been raging higher every time he'd seen her.

He'd arrived at her home earlier to find the girls with only their nanny. Kassandra had picked today to swerve from her unchanging timetable to catch up on the schedule he'd disrupted.

He'd been dismayed by her absence for about ten seconds. Then the girls had come running to meet him, making him glad instead that she wasn't there. He could have some time with them alone, savoring their unbridled eagerness for his presence without the searing upheaval of hers.

The nanny, who'd instantly recognized him from the constant media exposure he'd been suffering recently, had delightedly invited him in. Though it had been to his advantage, he'd at first been disturbed she had without consulting the lady of the house. However, his thorough research, which he subjected anyone who came near Kassandra and the twins to, had indicated she was impeccably trustworthy. Though in her case, Kassandra's implicit trust in her would have been enough to put his mind at ease.

But besides judging someone in his exalted position to be safe, the lady must have taken one look at him with Zoya and worked out with 100 percent certainty who he really was. Yet even if she'd let him in for all the right reasons, he still needed to have an aside with her about never assuming anything, always checking first with Kassandra. He had zero tolerance when it came to the security of this household.

Only one thing had made him lenient with her. The

girls' fervent welcome. He still couldn't believe its extent. It had been as if they'd been waiting for him all their lives. As he had been for them.

The only pursuit that had kept him sane had been monitoring their every breath, along with Kassandra's, in those endless months after his accident. He hadn't allowed himself to imagine, let alone hope, for anything like that. He hadn't even tried to extrapolate his own reactions to seeing and feeling them in the flesh.

To have them respond so…miraculously to him had been beyond belief. As for his own feelings, they were… beyond description. At times, beyond endurance. From that moment they'd so unbelievably given him their trust, he'd known. He wouldn't be able to live another day without either of them.

Tonight had been further proof the magic he'd experienced with them the night before hadn't been a fluke. By the time they'd climbed over him and fallen asleep in perfect synchronicity, as if they shared an off switch and had telepathically agreed to flip it simultaneously, he'd been beyond enchanted and overwhelmed. Then he'd felt Kassandra's approach. Long before he heard her garage door opening.

He'd been suddenly loath to face her, yet unable to do anything but clasp the girls and wait for her to initiate the confrontation. His heart now thundered in his chest like it had then. In tandem, his hip joint started to throb with a red-hot warning that he'd pay the price of these miles in shoes unfit for walking for days to come.

He would welcome the physical discomfort. If only it were potent enough to counter his emotional turmoil. But no amount of pain could do so.

He'd expected being near Kassandra again would be

hard. Horrible, even. It wasn't. It was unbearable. With every passing moment in her company, the corrosive longing he'd suffered since he'd pushed her out of his life had been escalating to all-consuming need.

After her initial rejection, she'd been evidently shocked at the twins' reaction to him, and at his handling of them. She'd surrendered to the necessity of putting up with him, for her—their—daughters' sake. But it was clear this was the extent of her concession. She wanted nothing more to do with him.

As she shouldn't. Even if she weren't so averse, he'd be the one to keep away. As he'd been exhausting himself trying to. Then he'd asked her to marry him.

He'd thought he'd braced himself for any response. But her horror had been so deep, so total, he'd scrambled to pledge every guarantee, offer every incentive to make the union worth her while. But it had only made things worse. Her desperation as she'd offered to lie to the whole world for as long as it took had made clear the depth of her abhorrence of him. Of anything that bound her to him, even a marriage in name only. Even if it made her a queen.

But how could he have expected any less? After the way he'd rejected and abandoned her? In the cruelest way, at the worst time?

And he'd only come back to add more injuries. He'd forced his way back into the life she'd struggled long and hard to make into an oasis of peace and stability for their daughters.

That moment she'd stepped back and told him to come into her home, into her life, he'd felt as if he'd been taken in after being out in the freezing cold forever. But that had only been an illusion. As it should be.

He didn't want her to take him back.

But though her extreme reaction to his proposal had proved she never would accept him, even for show, she hadn't moved on. She hadn't found another man to bless. She hadn't even let any near. During his painstaking surveillance, many, many men had approached her. Three had offered her everything a man could offer a woman, starting with their hearts. It pained him to admit it, but she wouldn't have gone wrong accepting any of them.

So why hadn't she?

Had she been so busy with work and the twins she'd had nothing left to offer, or want? Or was he responsible for her being unable to move on, for becoming defensive and distant, even with the people closest to her, when she'd been the most emotionally generous and approachable person he'd had the undeserved privilege to know?

Pushing her away after the accident, he'd known he'd hurt her. But he'd thought her pain would soon become anger, helping her get over it. Over him. He hadn't suspected she'd linger in perpetual purgatory. Like he had.

But if she couldn't move on, then he hadn't just hurt her. He'd crippled her. And this had only one explanation: her feelings for him had been much deeper than he'd suspected.

Now she'd distilled her entire existence to being the twins' mother. Even her business seemed to have become a means to financial independence for their sake. Success and achievement were by-products, not the goals they'd once been.

He couldn't bear to think he'd damaged her irrevocably. That just by being near her again, he'd cause her even more harm.

But…maybe he didn't have to. Maybe instead of being

a disruption to her peace and a threat to her psyche, he could instead be her support, her ally. Maybe in time, he could heal her. Enough so she could move on, find love and build a life for herself, as a woman, with another man.

Even if it would finish him off.

When Leonid arrived at Kassandra's office the next day, her PA didn't intercept him, only fumblingly gave her boss the heads-up she'd failed to give her at his first incursion.

This time Kassandra opened her office door herself, and stepped silently aside to let him in, making no eye contact.

As she turned to him, he began at once. "I know how inconvenient and unfair to you the whole situation is, and if it was up to me, I'd accept your alternative proposition without qualifications. I will, as soon as I make certain it would satisfy the twins' legal legitimacy requirements in my kingdom."

Pushing a swathe of hair that seemed to encompass a thousand golden hues behind her ear, her emerald gaze regarded him steadily. "Then, it's as good as accepted. I'm sure you can achieve anything."

He tried not to wince at the cold resentment in her eyes, and the hot pain in his hip. "If only that was true. But I'll need your help to authenticate our fictitious marriage."

Everything about her stilled. "What am I supposed to do?"

"You have to come to my homeland."

A dozen conflicting emotions raced across her face before she shrugged. "Once you 'legitimize' the girls and become king, if I have to sign or swear anything in front of kingdom officials, I'll come."

He shook his head in frustration at his inability to make this easier on her. "I need you there before the coronation."

That wary watchfulness gripped her again. "When is that?"

"If all goes well, in a month's time now."

Her lips fell open. "You mean you want me to go to Zorya in less than a month?"

"No, I don't mean that." Before she could relax her clenched muscles, he exhaled. "We have to leave to-morrow."

Six

By the time the limo stopped at the private airfield, Eva and Zoya were sound asleep. Kyria Despina had also nodded off. Kassandra's alertness and agitation had only intensified with every passing second.

They reached a screaming pitch when Leonid got out and came around to hand her out. His smile, more than the coldness of the night after the warmth of the limo, sprouted goose bumps all over her. Oblivious to his effect on her, he got busy releasing the girls' car seat harnesses, insisting on carrying both.

After gesturing for those awaiting them on the tarmac to take her and the groggy Despina's hand luggage and the cats' carriers, he led them up into the giant silver jet.

With many of her family and friends being billionaires, she'd been on private jets before. But she'd never been on one of Leonid's. That fact underlined the superficiality of their liaison. She'd been the one who'd made the fatal mistake of becoming deeply involved, breaking the rules they'd agreed on, as he'd accused her of.

But all the other jets were nothing compared to this one. It felt…royal. So was it Zorya's equivalent of Air Force One? That made sense. From the news, Zorya no longer considered Leonid a candidate, but the future king, the man who'd resurrect their kingdom and restore its grandeur. It was a fitting ride for a man of his stature and importance.

With his staff and the jet's crew hovering in the background, Leonid led them through many compartments to a spiral staircase to the upper deck. Once there, he walked them across an ultrachic foyer, then through an automatic door that he opened using a fingerprint recognition module. So no one was allowed past this point except him, and those he let in.

The door whirred shut behind them as he guided them to a bedroom with two double beds, two special cribs and a huge pet enclosure for the cats. He'd prepared the jet for them!

After she helped him secure the girls and cats, he showed Despina the suite's amenities and assured her she should settle down for a full night's sleep.

As he led Kassandra back outside, it dawned on her that, with the transcontinental flight, they'd be traveling all through the night. Alone together.

Even if she convinced him to sleep himself, so she'd be spared the turmoil of his company, she wouldn't be able to even close her eyes knowing he was so close by. But she doubted he'd sleep and leave her. Apart from that one time he'd been beyond observing decorum and had told her what he'd really felt, he'd always been terminally gallant. And since she'd agreed to go to Zorya, he'd been more courteous than ever. It was enough to make her want to scream.

Resigned to a night in the hell of his nearness, she sagged down on a cream leather couch. Forcing her attention off him, she looked around the grand lounge.

Dominated by Slavic designs, the room was drenched in golden lights and earth tones, embodying the serenity of sumptuousness and seclusion. At the far end of the space that occupied the breadth of the massive jet, a screen of complementing colors and designs obscured another area behind it.

"This—" he gestured to a door "—is the lavatory." Another gesture. "And those buttons access all functions and services in this compartment. Please order refreshments or whatever you wish for until I come back."

She almost blurted out that he *didn't* need to come back, that he should go tend to matters of state or something. But she remained silent as he paused at the lounge's door, his fathomless voice caressing every starved cell in her.

"I'll only be a few minutes."

Once he disappeared, she headed to the lavatory, just for something to do, and stayed inside for as long as she could bear.

Once she came out, she did a double take, and faltered, gulping air. He'd come back, and he'd taken off his...jacket!

Had he been naked, he probably wouldn't have affected her more. Okay, he would have, but it was bad enough now. And his clothes weren't even that fitted, just a loose and simple white shirt and black pants. If anything about him or what he provoked in her could be called simple.

He smiled that slow, searing smile he'd been bestowing on her again since yesterday. Unable to smile back, she approached him, her stamina tank running lower by the second.

He'd been supremely fit before, but the added bulk of his new lifestyle suited him endlessly. The breadth of his chest and shoulders that had never owed their perfection to tailoring felt magnified now that only a layer of finest silk covered them. They, and his arms, bulged with strength and symmetry. Yet his abdomen was as hard as ever, his waist and hips as narrow, making his upper body look even more formidable. She didn't dare pause on the area at the juncture of his powerful thighs.

And that was only his body. The body that had enslaved her every sense, owned her every response, had possessed and pleasured her for a whole year. The body whose essence had mingled with hers and created their twin miracles. Then came the rest. The regal shape of his head, the deep, dark gloss of his hair, the hewn sculpture of his face, the seductiveness of his lips, the hypnosis of his eyes.

If he'd been Hermes before, he was now Ares. If ever a man was born to lead, to be king, it was him.

He extended one of those perfect, powerful hands that had once treated her to unimaginable intimacies and ecstasies.

"Come sit down, Kassandra. We're about to take off."

She sat down where the tranquil sweep of his hand indicated. Before she collapsed. No longer the stiff stranger he'd been with her, the way he moved, sounded, smelled, breathed, the way he just *was*…

It was all too much.

Unaware that just being near, just being him, was causing her unbearable pain, he sat down on the seat opposite her couch. His descent was smoother than her flop, yet a frown shadowed his leonine brow. She could feel frustration radiating from him at his inability to move as effortlessly as before. After his previous preternatural litheness, it must be indescribably disconcerting to him to no longer have total control over his every move, to orchestrate them in that symphony of grace that he used to.

Getting his irritation under control with obvious difficulty, he secured his seat belt and pressed a button in his armrest. The engines revved higher and the jet started moving.

To escape the gaze he pinned on her again, she fastened her seat belt and examined the panel in her own armrest. She didn't get most of the functions. But then, in her condition, she wouldn't have recognized a neon exit sign.

If only this situation came with one. It didn't, not for the foreseeable future. If one ever became available, it wouldn't be called an exit, but an escape, with whatever could be saved. If anything remained salvageable this time.

For now, she couldn't even figure out what had happened since Leonid had said they had to go to Zorya in a day's time.

That statement had been met with her finest snort. But he'd been as serious as a tidal wave, inundating her objections. And as she continued to discover, resistance with him was indeed futile.

After he'd left, she'd done what he'd made her agree

to, called every person, agency and organization she'd made prior plans, signed contracts or had delivery dates with, to request extensions. Not expecting to get any, she'd felt secure that these commitments would be her excuse not to comply with his timetable.

But they'd all come back to her within hours, *offering* her all the time she wanted. Sans penalty. Some with an increase in compensation for her "extra time and effort."

Not only was she burning to know how he'd done that, but she was getting more anxious about what he'd done to achieve these unbelievable results.

But now that she was sentenced to a night of sleepless torture in his company, she was bent on getting some answers. She wouldn't let him escape her questioning again as he had so far, on account of being too busy preparing their departure.

She raised her gaze to him, found him studying her with yet another inscrutable expression in his incredible eyes.

Suppressing tremors of longing, she cocked her head at him. "Now that you have nowhere to go for the next fourteen hours, you will tell me."

His eyes maintained that enigmatic cast. "Who says I have nowhere to go? This jet has a depressurizing compartment in the rear so I can make a dash for it in extreme emergencies."

"And you consider this one? You'd skydive from forty thousand feet, at six hundred miles an hour, into the big unknown below, to escape telling me how you got all those multibillion-dollar enterprises to postpone my multimillion-dollar deals with a smile and a bonus on top?"

His eyes crinkled, filling with what she thought she'd

never see there again. Bedevilment. "If you saw the look in your eyes, you'd categorize this as a jump-worthy situation."

Pursing her lips to suppress the moronic urge to grin at him, when for the past two years plus he'd certainly caused her nothing to grin about, she plastered her best attempt at severity on her face. "What did you do, Leonid?"

His lips mimicked hers in earnestness, but the smile kept attempting to escape. "What do you think I did?"

"I have theories, and fears. Not in your best interests to keep me in suspense with that combustible mix."

A revving chuckle erupted deep in his endless chest. "I did mean it when I said I'd tell you when I had the time and presence of mind. But now that I realize you have all those theories and fears, I must hear them first. So you tell me what you think I did, and if it's close, I'll tell you the exact details."

Was he…teasing her? What had gotten into him? Where was the automaton who'd stood on her doorstep playing back what had sounded like a recorded script and programmed responses?

Was he practicing the ease they'd display as newly reconciled husband and wife? He had said polite formality would be fine in public, but what if he'd decided it was more effective to give his adoring subjects a doting couple to moon over?

In other modern kingdoms, the alleged love stories between royal couples counted as a major asset for the monarchy, contributing to its political and social stability. It was also a huge source of economic prosperity via revenues for the media and tourism machines.

So now that she'd accommodated all his demands and

he was no longer anxious about his plans, was he relaxing and rehearsing in preparation for giving the public a convincing performance?

Or was it even worse? Had he decided to enslave the world by reverting to his previous self, the one she'd fallen fathoms deep for, and hadn't been able to kick her way to the surface since?

Unable to even think of the ramifications to herself if this was the case, she focused on his current challenge, knowing he wouldn't reveal anything if she didn't meet it.

"It's not what I think as much as what I hope you did. For the future of my business, I hope there was no coercion or intimidation on your part, but that as a former world champion, current mogul and future king, you have endless strings to pull, gently, and that you binged on using all the favors you could."

Those perfectly arched eyebrows shot up. "And leave myself in a favor deficit as I embark on ruling a historically contested land with a nascent independence amidst a turbulent sea of cranky killer-whale and bloodthirsty-shark nations?"

When he put it that way, her worries didn't even seem relevant.

Shoulders drooping, she flopped back on the couch. "So my business was too small a fry for you to spend favors on, huh?"

He unbuckled himself, rose and came down beside her, much closer than his usual very long arm's length. "Actually, your business is a huge enough fish I didn't need to."

Her wits scattering at his action, his nearness, she tried to focus on the meaning of his words. And failed.

Giving up, she croaked, "What's that supposed to mean?"

"It means the only good my calls did was explain the time-sensitive nature of your request, since you didn't."

"What exactly did you tell them?"

"The truth, but I requested their discretion until we made a public announcement. But they were already falling over themselves to adjust their plans to accommodate your needs. I just told them you needed their response ASAP for your peace of mind before our trip and subsequent major events. All I did was make them call you sooner with their acceptance."

When she could only gape at him in disbelief, his lips crooked with what very dangerously resembled indulgent pride.

"I already knew how respected and valued you are, but today I discovered your popularity is phenomenal. You've built such a massive reserve of goodwill, such need for your name, products and collaboration, everyone said and proved they'd do whatever they had to for the opportunity to keep on working with you."

Finding this revelation too much to accept, she shook her head. "They must have hoped it would be a big favor to you. Who wouldn't want to be in your good graces?"

His pout was all gentle chastisement. "You don't know your own influence on people at all, do you?"

I used to have a pretty good idea. Until you pulverized my belief in my own judgment and my self-esteem.

But it wasn't time now, or ever, to voice that grievance.

"Even if some were willing to accommodate me, you have to be exaggerating such a sweeping response. It had to be *your* influence. They must have calculated that a point with you would appreciate astronomically. No advantage gained by rejecting my request would be worth being in your bad books."

Without saying anything further, he got out his phone, dialed a number. In seconds, the line opened.

"Signor Bernatelli…" He paused for a second as an exclamation carried to her ears from the other side.

Sergio Bernatelli, the top Italian designer she was collaborating with in her biggest project to date, had recognized his voice, or saved his number. Probably both.

"…yes, it's indeed fortunate to be talking to you again. Yes, we are on our way to Zorya." Another pause as the man bubbled over on the other side. "That would be totally up to Kassandra. Why don't you ask her? And can you please also repeat to her what you said to me when I called you earlier? Thank you, Signor Bernatelli, and look for our invitation to the coronation in the mail in a couple of weeks."

After she numbly took the phone from him, she barely got a hello in before the flamboyant man submerged her in his excitement about her upgrade to royal status, and his hopes she would consider him for a creation designed for her to wear to the coronation, or any royal function at all. Before she could express her gratitude for such a gift—though it would mean huge publicity for him— he repeated everything Leonid had told her, in his far more over-the-top language, which he usually reserved for blistering complaints and demolishing critique.

After she ended the call, she kept staring at Leonid, tingling with the incredible praise Bernatelli had lavished on her. Not only where it pertained to him and his design empire, but to the whole field.

"I trust you believe me now?" Leonid smiled expectantly.

She started to nod, but stopped. "Maybe not. Maybe knowing I'd ask, you put him up to this so he'd back your story."

Incredulity widened his eyes. "Following that reasoning, shouldn't I have picked an accomplice you'd be more inclined to believe would have such a glowing opinion of you? Why pick that cantankerous scrooge when praises from him would be the most suspicious?"

"Maybe that's exactly why you chose him, because it would have been too obvious to pick someone agreeable, and such a famed grouch's vote would carry more weight and credibility."

Leonid threw his hands up in the air, "*Bozhe moy*, Kassandra! That's too convoluted for even me. My brain is now starting to ache trying to contort around that pretzeled piece of logic."

She opened her mouth to confront him with another suspicion, but closed it. That was real bewilderment in his eyes. Worse, the levity that had been present all day, that she'd delighted in in spite of herself, was gone. She'd weirded him out because of her attack of dogged insecurity.

At her prolonged silence, he exhaled. "Did you only run out of arguments, but still believe in my deceit?"

Grimacing at how unreasonable she must have sounded, she sighed. "No, I believe you. But even if your calls only made a difference in timing, that's still a big thing. I would have been beside myself with worry if we left without hearing back from them. And because of your calls I learned something I wouldn't have on my own. People find it hard to say their opinions to someone's face, even if it's glowing praise. Or especially when it is. It's good to know I'm in such universal favor."

A relieved smile dawned on his heartbreakingly handsome face. "Which isn't a favor at all, but your due." He sat up, eagerness entering his pose. "And now that you realize your power, I'll counsel you on how to exercise it more effectively, to your benefit and that of the whole industry."

Her first instinct was to decline his offer. Then her mind did a one-eighty.

Why refuse? What made more sense than for her to accept the advantages of his invaluable insight and enormous experience, when it would be for everyone's benefit?

Suddenly, what she'd thought would never come to pass happened. She exchanged a smile with him, devoid of tension and shadows. Then the door to the bedroom opened.

Tousled and half-asleep on her feet, Despina stood in the door, carrying a very awake Eva and Zoya.

Leonid pushed to his feet before she could, his delight at seeing the girls blatant and unreserved. Their equal glee at finding him again manifested in excited shrieks as both of them flung themselves into his open arms.

Resigned that she was the old news they'd forgo until Leonid's novelty wore off, Kassandra sighed. "Sorry, Kyria Despina. I really thought they'd sleep through the night since they haven't woken up the past few days. Wonder if they're back to their habit, or if it's only today's different pattern and strange cribs that roused them."

"Why do you think they wake up?" Leonid asked.

"They seemed to hate letting go of all the fun they

were having before they sleep, wanting a few more hugs or another song or anything they were enjoying before they turned off."

Squeezing the girls tighter into his chest until their squeals became piercing, he laughed...*laughed*. "And there's plenty more of all of those things for *moy zvez-dochky*."

His starlets. This was his favorite endearment for them already. His morning and evening stars.

He used to have endearments for her, too. Mostly while in the throes of pleasure. *Moya dorogaya krasavista... moya zolotoya krasota... My beautiful darling...my golden beauty.*

She would never hear them from him again.

Now all his attention was diverted to the girls, and he looked as if he'd been given an unexpected second chance at something irreplaceable. Then he grimaced, turning his gaze to Despina.

"Kyria Despina, please go back to sleep. We'll keep them with us if they fall asleep again, so as not to disturb you."

Shaking off her dimming mood, Kassandra had to intervene. "Uh, I actually never let them wake up to find themselves outside their cribs. They're notorious for picking up bad habits once I break a pattern and it's a struggle going back to any sort of order."

Nodding his deference to her decree at once, he strode toward Despina. "Let me take you to another bedroom. I'm sorry to move you, but from now on your sleep will be uninterrupted when the twins wake up at night."

Despina rushed beside him, assuring him she didn't mind at all, her cheeks flushed by the pleasure of having a royal god like Leonid fussing over her.

Within moments, Leonid marched back with the girls, one straddling his shoulders, the other his waist. They babbled as he cooed to them. "Papa" was repeated profusely as both swamped him in hugs and kisses, with him looking utterly blissful as he reciprocated.

They looked agonizingly beautiful together.

But that agony dissipated as they joined her, and she was infected by their gaiety and pleasure at being together.

An hour later, long after they should have gone back to sleep, as they all sat playing in the sandbox that had been ingeniously hidden until Leonid had unveiled it, the toddlers started gnawing their fists and drooling.

Concern coated Leonid's magnificent face as they both rushed to clean the twins' hands, even if what passed for sand was totally safe. He looked at her. "They're in the molar eruption phase now, right?"

She was impressed. "Give the new daddy a star. You've done your homework, I see."

"Of course. But since they didn't display any of the usual signs of teething before, I almost forgot about it."

"Well, health-wise, the girls have been a dream. Even teething has been progressing without signs of discomfort."

"But they're almost gnawing their little hands off and drooling up a storm!"

She chuckled at his growing agitation, content to be the wise, experienced parent who kept a cool head. "Don't ask me why, but it's their current method of letting me know they're hungry. No, let me correct that. Starving."

His eyes lit up in relief. "Of course they are. I thought they ate so much less than usual during their dinner."

"They were too excited with all the preparations to eat."

"And it turned out to be the best thing they did. So they'd wake up and play with their papa, and let him feed them their first Zoryan meal. I'm ordering you a feast!"

His enthusiasm widened her grin as he reached for the panel in his chair. He'd explained he'd given that jet to Zorya, not the other way around, to be the monarch's jet, long before he knew it would be him.

Though she'd thought she wasn't hungry, by the time he opened the door to waiters holding trays high, her stomach rumbled. Loudly. The food aromas were distressingly delicious, and even the fussy girls were smacking their lips.

Grinning at their demonstration of hunger, he rose, held his hand down to her. She took it, but along with her own upward momentum, she ended up falling against him. For a moment, it felt as if a thousand-volt lash had flayed her where their bodies touched, from chest to hip.

It was he who pulled back first, almost anxiously, his eyes once more unfathomable. The moment passed as the girls scampered around, pulling at them to get on with feeding them.

Getting back into the flow of talking with Eva and Zoya with their system of English, Zoryan Russian and baby talk, he led them behind the screen she'd noticed before. Turned out there was a full dining area there, with gold-and-black silk-upholstered chairs. In the center stood an elaborate table decorated with Zorya's magnificently rendered and detailed emblem of the two goddesses.

As they sat down, Leonid explained to the girls that they were like those two goddesses, night and day twins. Zorya would consider them the symbol of its rebirth, just like the goddesses were responsible for its original birth. He enlisted Kassandra's help in simplifying the concept, and it all turned into a game as the girls caught on to the resemblance and imitated the goddesses' poses.

The food, which Leonid explained in detail, was beyond delicious. Even the usually picky girls devoured anything Leonid offered them. Kassandra insisted it had more to do with him doing the offering than the tastiness of the food itself.

Midmeal, the girls asked to sit in the place of the goddesses in the emblem. Getting her okay, Leonid improvised a new game, placing plates on the symbols surrounding the goddesses, offering them all forkfuls, and making Eva and Zoya laugh all the harder each time he theatrically dipped a fork in a plate and zoomed it toward a wide-open mouth, sometimes even Kassandra's.

She kept wondering how this had become the last thing she'd expected it to be—a delightful family trip. His new approachability and the girls' enthusiasm and spontaneity had dissolved the artifice and distance the past had imposed on them, revealing Leonid as he was now. He'd told the truth. He was no longer the man she'd loved, but far better, warmer, endlessly patient and accommodating, the perfect companion and the best father-in-training she could have imagined.

After they finished eating and the waiters had removed all signs of their meal, Leonid got the girls off the table and clapped. "How about some Zoryan music, *moy zvezdochky?*"

As if they understood, and maybe they truly did, the girls yelled in agreement. Once Leonid had the infectiously joyous music filling their cocoon of luxury, he started teaching the girls the steps of a Zoryan folk dance. Noticing how hard it was for him to execute even those simple steps, she studied them quickly and took over teaching them as best she could. Soon they were all dancing with Leonid watching them, keeping the tempo with powerful claps, singing along, his rich bass deepening the spell.

Whenever one song ended and another started, Leonid would urge them on. "*Tantsevat', moy prekrasnyye damy.* Dance!"

This time, he'd included her when he'd said "my beautiful ladies." At least she thought he'd included her.

But why should she doubt it? The whole day he'd gone above and beyond doting on both the girls and her. He'd given her the gift of showing her how important she was to her colleagues in her field. He'd been exemplary in recognizing her superior knowledge of the girls, had showed them in no uncertain terms that, though he was their papa who would do anything for them, it was mama who was the boss. He'd been plain magnificent to her.

When she said no more, he invited her down on the carpeted floor. They sat with their backs to the couch, with the girls climbing on and off them, bringing them toys and asking them to name them in their respective languages. Then she and Leonid quizzed them. To all their excitement, the girls remembered almost everything and said the words as accurately as possible in the three languages.

The games continued for hours. Then the girls suddenly lay down across his and her side-by-side bodies, making a bridge between them with theirs, and promptly fell asleep.

They remained sitting like this, sharing the connection their daughters had spontaneously created between them in serene silence for what could have been another hour, alternating caressing the girls' silky heads.

Suddenly, his black-velvet voice spread over her like a caress. *"Oni ideal'ny."*

She nodded, heart swelling with sudden, overwhelming gratitude. For them. And for him. "Yes. They are perfect." At length, she added, "Let's put them to bed."

Without objection, even when she could see he wanted to savor them for far longer, he gathered one girl after the other and rose with them in his arms.

On the way to their bedroom, she had to voice her wonder. "You'll have to show me how you keep them stuck to you like this when they're asleep. Either you're a literal babe magnet, or you three share some Voronov Vacuum quality."

A surprised huff of mirth escaped him before he suppressed it. Then he seemed to remember nothing could disturb them, and let it all out.

As they went back to the lounge, he was still chuckling as he put on a different kind of music, still Zoryan, but perfect for setting a soothing mood.

Sitting down on the couch, he suddenly guffawed again. "Voronov Vacuum. I should patent this."

She grinned her pleasure at his appreciation of her quip. "You should. That brand name is just meant to be."

He sighed, still smiling. "I wanted to ask you to let them sleep like that between us, as if laying claim to both of us. You know I lost my parents when I was not much older than they are, was raised by indulgent relatives. What you don't know is that I struggled to cultivate the discipline my parents would have instilled in me, had they lived. So I know how important it is to have structure in one's life, and I truly admire your ability to provide and maintain it. I will happily follow your lead and reinforce your methods." He signed even more exaggeratedly. "Even if the new papa in me wants to mindlessly indulge them to thorough and decadent rottenness."

She chuckled at his mock-mournful complaint. "You have a lifetime to indulge them, *and* discipline them, *and* the rest of the roller coaster of unimaginable ups and downs of parenthood to look forward to. Pace yourself. I'm trying to."

His eyes glittered with such poignancy, as if it was the first time he dared to let himself look forward that far. "I do have a lifetime, don't I? I am their father forever."

Throat sealing with emotion, she nodded. "If you want to be."

His azure eyes flared with such elation and entreaty. Then he only said a hoarse "Please."

The word rolled through her every cell like thunder. And everything inside her snapped.

Then she was pressing all she could of herself into what she could of him, lips blindly seeking every part of him she'd starved for, all her suppressed longing bursting out in a reiteration so ragged it was a prayer.

"Yes, Leonid, yes, please...*please*..."

Seven

Among the cacophony of her thundering heart and strident breathing, Kassandra heard a piece of music ending and a more evocative one starting. And she was pleading. Pleading. Pleading. For what, she didn't know.

But she *did* know. She was pleading for him. For them. For an explanation. A reconnection. A resurrection.

Just touching him again felt like coming back to life. If only he'd touch her back.

But he had frozen from the moment she'd obliterated the distance between them, had done what she'd been suffocating for since that moment she'd seen his crumpled car in the news. To touch him, feel him, reassure herself he was here and whole, that she hadn't lost him.

But she had lost him. He'd imposed his loss on her. But she now realized that through all the pain, there had remained the consolation that he still existed, that she hadn't lost him that way. In the depths of her soul, hidden from her pain and pride, there had always been the hope that maybe, one day, this meant she could have him back.

Now nothing mattered to her anymore but the fact that he was the only man she'd ever want, that he was her girls' father and he loved them. That he'd come back for them had shown her a glimpse of the perfection they could have.

Now all she wanted was for him to end her exile.

Her hands and lips roaming his solid vitality, singed by his heat, tapping into his life, she begged for his response.

Please. Please. Please.

Then he moved...away.

Her lips stilled on his chest, mortification welling inside her like lava. He was rejecting her again.

But...maybe not. With the debris of the past between them, he wouldn't presume to take what she was offering when he didn't know what it was, or how it would affect their sensitive situation and fragile new harmony.

But this wasn't the past. This was now. It could be their tomorrows. She had to risk new injury for the slightest possibility this new man he'd become had changed toward her, too, and might now want her as she wanted him. He had wanted her once, before he'd stopped. Maybe this time he wouldn't stop.

Pulling back to look up at him through eyes filling with tears, she found his face clenched as hard as the muscles that had turned to rock beneath her fingers, buzzed like live wires. He was shocked. And aroused as hell.

His hunger buffeted her, left her in no doubt. It wasn't lack of desire that made him pull back, but uncertainty.

Attempting to erase any doubts he had, she pressed against him, sobbed into his hot neck against his bounding pulse, "Take me, Leonid, just take me, *please…*"

"Kassandra…" His rumble of her name reverberated inside her as he heaved up, tugging her with him. In the past, he would have scooped her up, but she knew he couldn't now.

Her legs still almost gave out as he rushed her through compartments, past the dining area to another closed door. Behind it was a bedroom as big as the lounge, dominated by a king-size bed covered in gold-and-black satin. His bedroom.

Before she could use what was left of her coordination to stumble to the bed, he closed the door and pressed her against it, taking her face in both hands. In the pervasive golden light, his face was supernatural in beauty, reflecting the hurricane building up inside him. His blue-fire gaze was explicit with one question: Did she know what she'd be getting into when he let it break over her?

Feeling she'd crumble into ashes if it didn't, she cried out, "Leonid, I want it all with you…"

With a groan that sounded as if something had ripped inside him, his head swooped down and blocked out existence.

Then he was swallowing her moans of his name, giving her his breath, reanimating her as he growled hers inside her.

"Kassandra…"

It was like opening a floodgate. To the past. To that first kiss that had been exactly like that. A conquering; a claiming. Her breath fractured inside her chest as she drowned in his feel and scent and taste. As she had that first time, and for a whole year afterward. She'd only drowned in desolation, alone, after he'd cast her out.

But she *was* drowning again now. In kisses that tantalized her with only glimpses of the ferocity she needed from him. His hands added to her torment, gliding all over her, never pausing long enough to appease, until she writhed against him, whimpering for what she'd never and could never stop wanting. Everything with and from him.

But he wasn't giving her everything, as if still testing her, not sure how total her surrender was.

She dug her fingers into his shoulders. "Leonid... *please*, give me *everything* you've got."

His head rose for one suspended moment, long enough for her to see his shackles snapping, then at last, he clamped his lips down on hers, hard, hot branding. His tongue thrust deep, singeing her with pleasure, breaching her with need, draining her of moans and reason.

She took it all, too lost to pleasure him in turn. His absence had left a void that had been growing larger every day until she'd feared it would hollow her out, leaving only a shell. Now he was here again, filling the emptiness.

Pressure built in her eyes, chest and core. Her hands convulsed on his arms until he relented, pushed her blouse up and over her head, pulled her bra strap down, setting her swollen breasts free.

She keened with relief, with the spike in arousal. He had her exposed, vulnerable. Desperate with arousal. Shaking hands pressed her breasts together to mitigate their aching as everything inside her surged, gushed, needing anything he would do to her. His fingers and tongue and teeth exploiting her every secret, his body all over hers, his manhood filling her core, thrusting her to oblivion…reclaiming her from the void.

Tears flooded down her cheeks. "Don't go slow, Leonid… I can't wait, I can't…"

Leonid had to be dreaming.

It had to be one of those tormenting figments that had hunted him mercilessly every moment since he'd watched her stumble out of his hospital room. Kassandra couldn't be pressing into him, all that glorious passion and flesh, sobbing for him to take her. He couldn't be scenting her arousal, feeling it vibrating in his loins, hearing it thundering in his cells.

She couldn't want him still, after what he'd done to her.

Her teeth sank into his bottom lip, hard, breaking his flesh. The taste of his blood mixing with her taste, inflamed his every nerve. Her distress felt so real.

It *was* real, a firebomb of madness detonating inside him, blowing away the last of his disbelief, and his control.

He smashed his lips harder into hers, and her cry of relief, of exultation tore through him. The need to ram into her, ride her, spill himself inside her, with no finesse, no restraint, drove him. Her flesh buzzed with her distress beneath his burning hands. Her incessant moans filled his head.

She wanted an invasion. And he would deliver.

It had been so long without her…so agonizingly long. He'd thought it would be for the rest of his miserable life. But his banishment was suddenly over. She was taking him back when he'd thought it an impossibility.

And he would take her as she needed him to, binge on her, perish inside her.

He swept her off her feet and she arched deep against the door, making a desperate offering of her core, her breasts, her hands behind his head sinking further into his sanity, speeding his descent into delirium.

He fell on her engorged breasts, starving, took what he could of her ripened femininity, where his daughters had suckled, insane with regret that he hadn't been there to witness it. Tearing her skirt farther up in rough, un-coordinated moves, he spread her thighs wide around his hips. She thrashed, clamped him with her legs and need, her sobs sharpening. His distress just as deep, he held her with one arm, reached between her legs, pushed aside her soaked panties, opened her folds and shud-dered, on the brink of release just gliding his fingers through her fluid heat.

Drawing harder on one nipple, then the other, he rubbed two fingers in shaking circles over the knot of flesh where her nerves converged. Once, twice, then he felt her stiffen, that soon. He gritted his teeth, anxious for the music of her release, even if he suffered perma-nent damage hearing it.

She came apart in his arms, magnificent, abandoned, her cries fueling his arousal to the point of agony. His hands shook out of control as he freed himself, the antici-pation so brutal his grip on consciousness was slipping.

Fighting to focus, he snatched her thighs back around him, groaned as her wet heat singed his erection, even as her heavy-lidded gaze scalded the rest of him. Growl-ing something not even he understood, driven, wild, his fingers dug into her buttocks. Her breasts swelled more at his roughness, her hardened nipples branding his raw flesh even through his clothes.

His vision distorted over lips swollen from his ferocity, quivering from a taut-with-need face. "Come inside me n—"

He drove up into her, roaring her name. But though molten for him, she was as tight as ever, her flesh resisting his invasion as he stretched her beyond her limits. But knowing their impossible fit only drove her beyond coherence with pleasure, he pulled out only to thrust back, again, then again, again, again, to the rhythm of her piercing screams as she consumed him in her velvet inferno, until he'd embedded himself inside her to the hilt.

Then he stilled in her depths, surrendered to her clenching hunger as it wrung him, razed him. At last. *At last.*

He rested his forehead against hers, overwhelmed, transported, listening to her delirium, to his. Her graceful back was a deep arch, granting him total freedom with her body.

Then it was no longer enough. The need to conquer her, finish her, end inside her rose like a tidal wave, as it always had, crashing and destroying everything, before building again as if it had never dissipated.

Blind, out of his mind, he lifted her, filled his mouth and hands with her flesh. He had to leave no fiber of her being unsaturated with pleasure. He withdrew all the way out of her then thrust back, harder, then harder still, until he was hammering inside her to the cadence he knew would overload her, until she convulsed in orgasm, her satin screams echoing his roars as he followed her into the abyss of pleasure.

Her convulsions spiked in intensity at the first splash of his seed against her womb, and he felt her heart spiraling out of control with his as a sustained seizure of release destroyed the world around them.

Then it was another life, where nothing existed except being merged with her, riding the aftershocks, savoring the plateau of ecstasy, sharing the descent.

It had been beyond control or description. Everything.

Yet it wasn't enough. Would anything with Kassandra ever be?

He knew the answer to that. Nothing ever would. He'd never had enough of her. He'd been hers alone since that first time he'd laid eyes on her. He would have remained hers even if he'd never had her again. Even if she'd hated him forever.

But defying comprehension, she didn't. Not only didn't she hate him, not only did she still want him, she seemed to have forgiven him. She'd given him her body again, her acceptance, her support with the twins, her ease. Her laughter. How was it even possible?

And he realized. *He'd* done that. When he hadn't meant to.

All he'd meant when he'd let go of the act of stiffness and distance had been to end her fears toward him, neutralize her hostility, for her own peace of mind. He hadn't dreamed she would not only relinquish her rightful hatred of him but seek his intimacy again, and with this unstoppable urgency.

And he realized something else. Even though she'd completed her descent from the peak of pleasure, she wasn't pulling away.

He withdrew a bit, keeping them merged as he looked down at her. She seemed disoriented, her eyes slumberous, fathomless as they gazed up at him. A goddess of temptation and fulfillment, something every man dreamed of but never really expected to find. And he'd found her, not only once, but against all odds, twice.

Unable to stop himself, his hands dug into her buttocks, gathering her tighter to him.

Her eyes scorched him to the bone with the amalgam of pleasure and pain that transfigured her amazing beauty as he expanded even more inside her. Her core, molten with their combined pleasure, contracted around him, making him thrust deeper into her, wrenching moans from both their depths. Then slowly, her lids slid down.

In seconds her breathing evened. She'd fallen asleep.

Overwhelming pride that he'd pleasured her so completely, as he'd used to, it had literally knocked her out, burgeoned inside him. He hardened even more, that first explosive encounter only serving to whet his appetite. As it always had, during their past extended sessions of delirium. Visions assailed him, of taking her to bed, making love to her again as she slept, until she woke up on another orgasm.

But he couldn't do that. He had to let her sleep.

Cursing his shoddy coordination, he gathered her in his arms and walked slowly with her precious weight. She'd left it all to his power in lax trust, testing his precarious balance. The trek to the bed felt endless. Placing her under the covers and adjusting her clothes, she stirred only to touch what she could of him with sleepy kisses and caresses, murmuring wonderful little incoherencies in appreciation of his caresses and coddling. He struggled up, heart thundering, brow covered in cold sweat. His control had one last notch before it slipped again.

One thing pulled him back from the temptation. The sheer regret and despair that pulverized the heart he'd thought had shriveled the day he'd pushed her away all over again.

This had been a terrible mistake.

For her sake, from now on, he had to leave her alone.

He couldn't succumb to her need, or his weakness, ever again.

Kassandra woke up from an inferno of eroticism, on fire.

Gasping as her dream about Leonid evaporated and with it the impending orgasm he'd been about to give her, it took her a disoriented minute to realize where she was. In Leonid's luxurious jet bedroom, fully clothed and tucked beneath covers that felt alive with silky touches and sighs.

Leonid had knocked her out with pleasure. As he'd always done. So even this hadn't changed.

Barely able to move, she turned her head to squint at the digital clock pinned down on the bedside table… and gasped. It was seven hours since she'd shut down in his arms. They must be about to land. And he must have had things to attend to. Which was a good thing. She didn't know how she would have faced him after what she'd done.

She'd almost attacked him in her arousal!

But once he'd made sure he knew what she'd been asking for, how far she'd wanted him to go, he'd…devastated her. She felt…ravished. Every inch of her felt fully exploited, delightfully sore and was screaming for an encore. Pushing away the covers that suddenly felt filled with hot thorns, she teetered barefoot to the adjoining bathroom.

It turned out to have a whirlpool tub, which she couldn't rush to fast enough, taking her clothes off to sink in.

As the warm currents bombarded her ultrasensitive flesh, her condition worsened as the memories of her encounter with Leonid boiled over in her blood. If he'd been here, she would have lost her mind all over again, and again.

When she couldn't take it anymore, she heaved out of the water and headed on trembling legs for the mirror, in front of which she shakily dried herself. She looked exactly like what she was. A woman who'd been possessed and pleasured within an inch of her sanity, and was now looking wild with her need for more.

But…would there be more? What would he say and do when she next saw…

"We are now approaching Zvaria, and will be landing in ten minutes. Please fasten your seat belts."

The pilot's announcement pulled her out of her feverish musings. But before she could head for the door, it opened. And she found herself face-to-face with Leonid.

Before her next heartbeat, he smiled, but it was detached, impersonal.

"Good, you're awake." Before she could respond, he opened the door wider. "Let's join the twins and share this historic event of landing in the Zoryan capital for the first time together."

As she approached him, he receded to let her pass. She tried to meet his eyes, read in them his response to what had happened between them, where he thought they'd go from there.

But he turned his gaze away in what seemed like a natural move as he invited her to lead the way.

Heart thudding to the rhythm of uncertainty and mortification, she walked ahead, her thoughts tangling.

Did he have too much on his mind, with the resolution of their situation and his looming responsibilities? Or was he just regretting what had happened?

Trying to project the ease she'd perfected for the girls' sake, she pinned a brittle smile on her face as they joined the others. As usual, Eva and Zoya demanded his attention, and hers to a lesser degree, leaving no room to focus on anything but them until they landed.

By the time they did, she'd decided she wouldn't torment herself with conjectures, that she'd let Leonid tell her what he thought and wanted when he had time for her alone again.

The moment she stepped out of the jet behind Leonid, who was carrying the girls, frosty air flayed her face and filled her lungs, so crisp and clean it made her gasp. The winter-wonderland vista beyond what was clearly another private airfield, with the imposing Carpathian Mountains in the distance, was so different from anywhere she'd ever lived, or even visited, that it reinforced again that she was a world away from her normal life in every sense.

She didn't have time to marvel at the awe-inspiring surroundings, or to linger over the realization that this rugged land must be responsible in part for Leonid's uncompromising distinctiveness. Her attention was drawn instead to the multitude of reporters and photographers who came literally out of left field to gather around the bottom of the stairs.

Her every hair stood on end as Leonid, who'd secured both girls in one arm, reached for her with the other one, posing for their first-ever family picture.

Then, as they resumed descending the stairs, the girls clung to him, burying their faces in his chest, eyeing the dozens of strangers calling out a cacophony of questions. Feeling his heat and power surrounding her, she found herself instinctively seeking his protection, too, dimly realizing what a sight they must make. The proud lion king, literally, with his pride of clinging females.

Leonid paused at the last step of the stairs and addressed the crowd. "Thank you for coming to meet my family, but you will understand that after the long flight, my only priority is their comfort. Each of you will get invitations to the press conference I will hold to answer all your questions as soon as my family is settled in their new home."

The reporters still tried to get him to say more, their voices rising with dozens of queries.

Leonid chose to answer one. "I do believe my daughters, Eva and Zoya, represent new life for our kingdom. They are literally that for me."

Brooking no further interruptions, he strode ahead and even the most dogged reporters parted before him as if unable to stand being in the path of his power.

Within minutes, they were seated inside a gleaming black stretch limo with the Zoryan flag flapping at the front.

She sat beside Leonid with the girls in their car seats facing them and Despina beside them. Leonid focused almost exclusively on the girls all the way to the palace, pointing out landmarks on the way and explaining their significance and history, with the girls appearing to take absolute interest in everything he brought to their attention and gleefully repeating the words he emphasized. Kassandra just kept telling herself to stick to her decision not to analyze his behavior, to stop thinking altogether.

Then they entered the palace complex grounds and all thought became impossible as she plunged ever deeper into the unreality of it all.

She'd been to the world's grandest palaces, as a tourist. Entering this place as a future resident, if things went according to Leonid's plan, was something else altogether. With the massive grounds populated by only those who worked there, it felt totally different from all the other palaces that had been crawling with visitors.

"This place was first laid out on the orders of Esfir the First, Zorya's founder and first queen." Her gaze swung to Leonid, and he gestured to her to look back at their surroundings as he continued narrating its history. "Her name, the Russian variant of Esther, also means *star*. This complex of palaces and gardens are sometimes referred to as the Zoryan Versailles. The central palace ensemble had been recognized as a UNESCO World Heritage Site since the fall of the Soviet Union and its return to the Zoryan state."

As she took in the information, he pointed toward another landmark. "The dominant natural feature is this sixteen-meter-high bluff lying less than a hundred meters from the shore of the Sea of Azov, which is part of the Black Sea. The Lower Gardens, or *Nizhny Sad*, encompassing over a square kilometer, are confined between this bluff and the shore. The majority of the complex's fountains are there, as are several small palaces and outbuildings. Atop the bluff, near the middle of the Lower Gardens, stands the Grand Palace, or *Bolshoi*

Dvorets, where the monarch historically resided...which
I'm now repairing and renovating, so I hope you'll excuse any mess. Ah, here is one of my favorite features
of the place..."

Kassandra's head swung to where he was pointing,
the most glorious cascade and fountain she'd ever seen,
situated right on the bluff's face below the body of a palace so grand it looked right out of a fairy tale.

"That's the Grand Cascade, or *Bolshoi Kaskad*, with
the Grand Palace forming the centerpiece of the entire
complex, and it's one of the most extensive waterworks
of the Baroque period."

Leonid kept explaining and describing what they were
passing through, with all of them, including the girls,
hanging on his every word. Apart from realizing he was
telling them important things he wanted them to learn,
the girls, like every other living being, she suspected,
just loved listening to his voice and were hypnotized by
the way he spoke.

The hypnosis only deepened as Leonid took them
inside what he kept referring to as their "new home."

In her jumbled state, Kassandra's mind couldn't as-
similate the details her eyes were registering, just the
major strokes. From beneath the scaffoldings of in-
progress renovations clearly close to being finished,
she could see an entrance, staggering in size and grandeur, under hundred-foot, painted dome ceilings, halls
with soaring arches with dozens of paintings depicting
naval battles, atmospheric landscapes and royal ances-
try, and chambers displaying countless ethnic influences
in their art and decor.

What made her focus sharpen were an inner garden
and pool that, while they had elements of the rest of the

place, were evidently new, and the most incredible parts of the palace to her. Somehow she had no doubt they were Leonid's idea and taste.

Throughout the tour, the girls, who'd never been in an edifice of that size, ran around squealing and pointing out their discoveries to interrogate Leonid about before another thing distracted them.

"And here are your quarters, for now."

They entered through white-painted, gold-paneled double doors to the most exquisite, expansive living area she'd ever seen. Though the dimensions and architecture echoed the rest of the palace, the furnishings and decor were more modern, comfort inducing and closely resembling the style and color scheme of her own living room in LA. And it was also outfitted and proofed for toddlers, clearly with Eva and Zoya in mind.

She wouldn't even ask how and when he'd had such personalized furnishings installed. He was powerful and rich enough he could have anything realized as soon as he thought of it.

But one thing didn't make sense. "For now?"

His smile didn't reach his eyes. "This is my effort at anticipating your needs and preferences. But you may decide you'd prefer some other place in the palace, or want something built on the grounds from scratch to your demands. So this will do until then."

"You can't seriously think I wouldn't find this perfect? It's actually...too much. This living *room* is as big as my whole place, which is big to start with. And I see glimpses of more tennis court–size rooms beyond."

He shrugged dismissively. "Everything is built on a grand scale in Zorya, even peasant's houses. You'll get used to it."

Will I? Will I also get used to you blowing searing then arctic, to never knowing where I really stand with you?

She only tossed her head toward Despina and the girls, who were rushing about exclaiming at all the delights he'd layered the place with. "Even if this magnificent place for some inexplicable reason didn't suit my taste, the girls and their nanny have given it their fervent seal of approval."

His lips twisted fondly before his eyes returned to hers earnestly. "I hope I thought of everything you might need, but you already met Fedor and Anya during our tour, my valet and his wife. Anya will be at your service for any domestic needs, and Fedor for anything else. Always call *me* first, with anything serious, even if I'm occupied with state emergencies. But Anya and Fedor are always ready for immediate and trivial matters." She nodded and he walked away. Midway to the door, he turned again. "You promise you *will* call me if you need anything?"

Heart expanding at his solicitude, shriveling at his withdrawal, she knew he'd wait until she said, "I promise."

Once he was gone, she rushed to the nearest bathroom and locked herself in. And let the tears flow. For she'd just promised she'd call him if she needed anything.

Anything but him. When he was all she needed.

Eight

Leonid stared at his reflection in the bathroom mirror.

He looked like hell. Much like he had in those days after he'd sent Kassandra away. He'd been keeping her away since they'd come to Zvaria three days ago. Every hour, every minute, every *second* had been sheer torture. Total chaos.

Every moment had been dedicated to concocting legitimate ways to escape being alone with her, so he wouldn't be forced to clarify his position. It had been getting progressively harder, with him perpetually on the precipice of doing something totally insane or irrevocably damaging. Or both. Like taking her against the nearest vertical surface, as he'd done back on the jet.

And he'd run out of excuses, could no longer run from a confrontation. Doing so could cause the very damage he'd been trying to avoid.

So he hadn't disappeared after they'd put the twins to bed. He was sure she would come after him. He could feel her drawing nearer, his every cell rioting with her proximity.

And he had no idea about what to say or do. None.

Severing the visual clash with his own bloodshot eyes, he stiffly moved away from the mirror, shuffled back to his reception area and sank down on an armchair facing the door. Counted down the heartbeats that would bring her to him with an infallible certainty. The soft knock on the door came as his countdown ran out. Though expected, it still juddered through him. His nerves were shot, his resistance depleted. At any point in this encounter, if she touched him, he would devour her.

Unable to rise again, he called out thickly, "Come in."

She'd realize he knew it was her. Who else would his guards allow to walk up to his quarters at this hour, or at all?

Bracing himself, his nerves still fired in unison when he saw her. That magnificent creature that had occupied his every waking and sleeping thought since he'd first laid eyes on her. In that deep burgundy floor-length dress she'd worn earlier tonight for dinner, which accentuated her complexion and curves. With her thousand-shade golden waterfall of silk and green-meadow eyes, she looked as magical as always. And as haggard as he did.

Without closing the door behind her, she approached, her gaze stripping away what was left of his tatters of control.

Thankfully, she didn't come close enough to test his nonexistent resolve. She started without preamble.

"I could pretend I didn't still want you when I was

angry with you, when I was afraid of you. But even before I quit being either, I admitted it to myself first, then to you on that jet. I do want you, more than ever."

He stared at her. He'd expected outrage, scolding, blame, anything but this confession.

She went on, "I know we agreed on a plan, and I haven't changed my mind about it. You tell everyone whatever would be best for you, the girls and your kingdom, and I'll back it up. I know you'd prefer to be together only for the girls, and I realize you haven't said a word about what happened between us on the jet because you're uncertain how to handle it. But I'm here to tell you that you don't need to overthink it or feel anxious about it. If your response to me wasn't just a random male one, if you want *me*, I am asking you not to hold back out of worry for your other considerations. Let's have this. Let's be together. No strings, no expectations. Just like in the past."

Then she fell silent, the brittle hope in her gaze shattering what remained of his sanity, and his heart. He struggled to force himself to remain still, expressionless, but inside him, a hurricane raged.

How was it possible she could offer him this? Not knowing his reasons for taking everything she had, in the past and recently, then throwing it in her face, she would be a masochist, a victim, to offer him a second, and now a third chance. Which she wasn't.

So did she want him so much that she was convincing herself his reasons were justifiable? Or was it even worse? Did she love him? In the past, and still now? Was she, after this magical trip to Zorya, and their explosive episode of passion, ready to expose herself to further injury for the chance of resurrecting something she shouldn't believe had ever been real?

It overwhelmed him, agonized him, that her feelings for him could be so fierce and profound they'd survived his humiliation, his desertion. When he had to let her down, again. And for the last time.

Even though it would leave him bloodied and extinguished.

But he was still unable to rebuff her, hurt her like that again. He had to try to soften the blow any way he could.

Feeling he'd be cutting off a vital part of himself with a jagged blade all over again, he started, "I doesn't matter what I want…"

Her stepping closer stopped him, and her tremulous objection twisted the knife hacking his guts. "It's all that matters. This isn't the past. Things have changed. You have. I have, too, along with things between us and everything else. We should be together for the sole reason that we want each other."

Feeling he was drowning, a breath away from heaving up and crushing her in his arms, begging for anything for as long as she would give it, come what may, he shook his head.

"You're right, this isn't the past. It's far worse. In the past, when I messed up, I hurt only you. Not that that was any less significant, or any more forgivable, but it remains a fact the damages I caused were limited to you. You've contained any repercussions for the twins so far with your strength and resourcefulness, aided by their young age. But now the situation is exceedingly more complicated. Personal considerations are the last thing to feature in my worries, and any damages would ripple out into widespread destruction."

Another urgent step brought her closer, her incredible beauty alight with passion. "That's what I meant by no expectations. There would be no repercussions to your kingdom or your relationship with the girls no matter what happens between us."

Destroyed by her offer of carte blanche, hating himself and the whole world even more for being forced to do this, her next words cleaved the remaining tatters keeping his heart in place.

"I've been thinking back to the time of your accident. Just before it happened, I was starting to feel restless. You were right when you thought I wanted to change the rules of our liaison. Though it wasn't premeditated, as you had believed. And contrary to what you thought, I wanted to negotiate, not for strings, but for more freedom. Our secrecy imposed too many barriers and limitations, and I wanted to be free of those, not to suggest different shackles. But when I saw your crumpled car, I knew then I only wanted you alive and well. That if I could only have you again, any way at all, I'd never want anything more. That feeling came back to me on the way here, made me face that I prefer the way it ended a million times to having it end...*that* way. And now I can't bear the possibility of missing out on being with you because I didn't let you know how I feel."

He looked away, unable to bear her baring everything inside her to him like that. He wasn't worthy of her courage and generosity, deserved none of her pure and magnificent emotions.

But escaping her gaze only brought her closer, until she touched him. Burned him to the marrow with one gentle, trembling caress on his shoulder.

"All that time, after you said you didn't want me anymore, what hurt most was the confusion, the disbelief. I couldn't imagine that what I felt from you, and so powerfully, didn't exist. Now everything inside me tells me what I felt from you back on the jet wasn't just sex. So please, Leonid…" Her cold, trembling hand cupped his jaw. It clenched so hard he was worried he'd grind his teeth to dust. "Tell me the truth. If you tell me you don't want me now, I'll walk away and this time I'll keep my distance and will never bring it up again. Just tell me, and I promise you, it won't change anything for you."

Tell her you don't want her. Set her free.

But he couldn't look at her and tell another such terrible lie. He couldn't watch the last embers go out in her eyes, and be replaced by the darkness of his final letdown.

Unable to breathe, praying he'd suffocate, cease to exist, he escaped the brutality of her gossamer touch, pitched forward, elbows crashing on his knees and head in his hands.

"Was this my mistake, then and now? Showing you how I feel? Was that what put you off?" And there they were. The tears she'd been holding at bay, soaking her voice as she entreated him one last time. "Leonid?"

He shook his head. Shook, period.

She made no sound, no gasp or whimper or sob. Even her steps were soundless. Yet her anguish as she silently left him was deafening, almost rupturing his head.

He'd hurt her irreparably and unforgivably again.

But now more than ever, now that he knew the sheer extent of her emotions, he knew he'd made the right decision. In the past and now. It was better to push her away, have her hate him, hurt her temporarily…than to do so permanently.

* * *

Kassandra walked through the majestic halls and corridors of the palace, afraid she'd scatter apart if she went any faster.

But she had to hold it together until she reached her quarters. Apart from the eyes that she felt were looking at her disapprovingly and pityingly from those lofty portraits, other hidden ones were monitoring her progress. Leonid's invisible security detail.

Not that they should be worried about him. Their future king was impervious. And lethal. As he should be, as he'd just explained he had to be, to be king.

The distance to her quarters seemed to have doubled. And they weren't her quarters. They were just the place Leonid had exiled her to across the massive palace. Now she knew beyond a doubt why. She had known since the first night he'd avoided her, but just had to make him stab any hope she'd been wrong to death.

Not that she could blame him this time. She'd taken a gamble that there was something between them, something old to resurrect or new to nurture, and she'd lost. She'd thought the slightest possibility she was right had been worth any price she'd have to pay if she turned out to be totally wrong. As she had been.

Leonid didn't want her. That incendiary encounter had been an unspecific response of an overendowed male to a female in heat. And he was clearly disgusted with himself for succumbing to a base urge he feared would jeopardize his priorities: his relationship with the girls, and his position as a king reestablishing a struggling monarchy.

And though it devastated her that she wasn't one of the things he cared about, she understood. He couldn't help how he felt, and how she felt wasn't his problem. He owed her nothing, but owed the girls and his kingdom everything.

So now she had to live up to her promises. Live close to him for her girls' sake, for his kingdom's, playing her expected role for the world, while showing him nothing but neutrality and pleasantness. Even as she withered with futile yearning for him forever. As she would.

In spite of everything, she'd never stopped loving him.

No. It was far worse that that.

Inexplicably, she loved him now more than ever.

"You were married all this time, let us suffer through the scandal of your pregnancy, and you want me to calm down?"

Kassandra winced. Her father's booming voice was loud enough it actually made the phone vibrate in her hand. Not to mention her brain shudder in her skull.

"Hush, Loukas, as if this is important anymore." That was her mother on the other line of a five-way video call.

It had taken Kassandra four days after her last confrontation with Leonid to call her family, who mainly lived in New York but for two exceptions, to explain the whole situation and invite them to the coronation in three weeks' time.

Only four out of the seven who made up her immediate family had been available. Her other two older brothers and another older sister texted to say they'd call as soon as they could. Now she was talking to her parents and two of her siblings.

"But Leonid Voronov... Now, *that's* the relevant thing here!" her mother exclaimed. "How were you even able to hide your relationship? Hide *him*?"

Kassandra sighed. Leave it to her parents to each fix-ate on what they considered the issue here. Her father felt she'd shamed him socially for nothing, and would now make him look like the oblivious father his daughter had ignored in choosing a husband, and her mother was questioning her gossiping network and her own secret-divining prowess.

"What's not making sense to me is that your breakup clearly happened after his accident." That was her old-est sister, Salome, married with four kids and living in Greece since her marriage. "The Kassandra we all know wouldn't have left the man she loved, at least loved enough to marry and submit to those convoluted cloak-and-dagger shenanigans to accommodate his desire for secrecy, when he'd just had a major accident."

"Can't you see you just answered your own ques-tion?" That was Aleksander, her year-younger brother, and almost her twin. "Voronov was the one who broke it off."

"But why, for God's sake?" Salome exclaimed as she rushed to stop her youngest, a four-year-old tornado by the name of Tomas, from dragging her laptop off the countertop. "At the time when he must have needed you most, when you needed to be with him…!" She put her son on the ground and focused back on her. "Say, it was around that time you discovered you were pregnant with the girls, wasn't it?"

She'd already resigned to spending this conversation answering questions, and sighing. As she was now. "I found out just before his accident."

"So he broke it off before you told him?" That was her father again, his voice like rumbling thunder. When she hesitated, he exploded. "He *knew* and still broke it off? And he's back now expecting you to forgive him and give him every right to the girls? I don't care who he is or who he's going to be, this man doesn't deserve to come near my daughter or granddaughters, and I'll see to it that he doesn't! I'll kill him first!"

"Baba…" Kassandra parroted her siblings' similar groans.

"Loukas!" her mother intervened. "You will calm down right this second. You're not going to kill anyone, starting with yourself. I forbid you to have another coronary!"

Kassandra's heart kicked. "Coronary! When was that?"

"See what you did, Rhea?" her father grumbled, looking like a petulant grizzly. "We agreed we wouldn't tell her. Now she'll worry herself silly when it was just a minor thing."

"Minor?" her mother huffed furiously. "You call multiple balloon catheters and stents minor? How about keeping me on my feet and dashing around for days as you whined and grouched and made impossible demands until I literally dropped? Still minor?"

"Don't mind them, Kass." Aleks chuckled, the mellowest male in their pureblood-Greek clan, and the one who'd been fully Americanized. Almost. "They're both back to peak condition, as you can see *and* hear, so don't even start asking what happened. Their tempers have been more hair-trigger than usual since that hospital stay and we won't be able to get them to stop if they start another episode in their Greek-tragedy love affair."

Aleks had always joked that their parents' dramatic fights were their way of spicing up a forty-plus-year marriage.

Looking positively murderous, her father glared at

his son, then turned to her. "I'm bringing your uncles and cousins, even those from your maternal side, to take care of this man."

"Whoa, you're deeming to enlist my brothers' and their progeny's help?" Her mother scoffed. "After forty-three years, they're finally good for something, in your opinion?"

Ignoring his wife, her father focused his wrath on Kassandra. "Russian king or billionaire or mobster or whatever that Voronov guy is…"

"He's actually Zoryan, not Russian," Aleks piped up.

"*Whatever* he is," their father shouted to drown out his youngest son's bedeviling, "we're teaching him a lesson about being a man, one he won't forget in this lifetime."

Kassandra's sigh was her deepest yet. "Congratulations, Baba. Now that you've detailed your plan to cause an international incident, you just made me revoke your invitation to the coronation."

Paternal thunder broke over her again, making everyone grimace and groan. "You're protecting him? He came back to you with puppy-dog eyes and all is forgiven? Not in my book. He needs to know the kind of consequences he faces when he messes with the Stavroses and their own."

"So you're drafting the Papagiannis in your war, but they don't even get mentioned in the credits?" Her mother snorted.

Salome raised her hand like a student seeking to be heard in a raucous class. "Didn't you notice the little detail that he came back with something more than a wagging tail? He's making your granddaughters princesses and your daughter a queen, for God's sake." She turned her eyes to Kassandra, the implication clearly just sinking in. "Oh, God, I can't wait to tell everyone here we're going to be European royalty!"

"Is Zorya a European kingdom, or is it counted as Asian?" Aleks mused the pragmatic curiosity on purpose, Kassandra was sure, to amplify her father's fury.

Ignoring him, Loukas Stavros leveled a glare at his firstborn, as if Salome had just called him a dirty name to his face. "I care nothing about what he offers. My granddaughters and daughter are already princesses and a queen without him."

Aleks chuckled. "As are all girls to their fathers, especially Greek fossils. Lighten up, Baba, this is the twenty-first century and your daughter is a world-renowned celebrity and businesswoman. She can take care of herself."

"And I *don't* care what she is to the world. To me, she is and will remain my little girl and I'll take care of her as long as there's breath in my body."

"You won't have many of those left if you keep hollering like that," her mother grumbled.

Kassandra raised her hand. "I knew I'd regret telling you anything, so thanks, everyone, for proving me right." She turned her gaze to her father. "If taking care of me means bringing the Stavros and Papagianni testosterone mob to Zorya to ambush Leonid, I'll have immigration revoke your visas at the airport and send you back on the first flight home."

Eyes widening at her threat, knowing she didn't make them lightly, her father pretended to laugh. "You're worried we're going to rough him up or something, *nariy kyria*? Nah, we'll just take him aside and...convince him of the error of his ways. I'm sure he'll be a better husband and father after our talk. This is men's stuff, so leave it to the men."

"Fine." As her father's face started relaxing, macho triumph coating his ruggedly handsome face, Kassandra added, "I'll have them send you home with heavily armed escorts from the CIA and its Zoryan equivalent."

Before her father went off again, she raised her voice, looking at her mother and sister. "About the estrogen posse… I'll leave instructions that the authorities are to sift you from your male components and let you through. But *only* if you promise you won't ambush Leonid yourselves, if for other purposes."

Salome burst out laughing. "After seeing the latest footage of him on the news today? No promises."

Her mother chuckled in agreement. "Don't be stingy. Let the women have some crumbs of your fairy-tale king. You're going to have, *and* eat, his whole cake, forever."

After that overt innuendo, her parents left the conference call to continue their argument in private. Her siblings had dozens of questions for her, each according to his or her interests.

She detailed the hectic preparations for the coronation, and the sweeping changes Leonid was implementing as he transitioned Zorya back to a sovereign state and kingdom. But whenever Salome asked about their relationship, she steered the conversation to Leonid's blossoming relationship with the girls. She wasn't about to tell her sister she'd resigned herself to a lifetime of co-parenting the girls with Leonid as polite strangers.

Not that that was accurate. He wasn't one. She had no idea what he was, had been going insane, constantly exposed to the suppressed emotions and hunger that blasted out of him.

Either she was imagining it, or what she sensed was real. But even if it was, by now she knew he had made up his mind never to act on those feelings, had zero hope he ever would.

For now, she managed to end the call without letting her siblings suspect this whole thing was the furthest thing from a fairy tale, or even an actual reconciliation. Or that she'd never been more miserable, hopeless and confused in her life.

She'd resigned herself to being so for the rest of her life. For the girls, and for the larger-than-life destiny she by now believed was their birthright.

Later that night, after disappearing all day, Leonid materialized like clockwork to have dinner with her and the girls, and to share in all their nightly rituals.

After they put their daughters to bed, he headed out of the wing, saying little, seeming anxious to leave her, alone and unappeased on every level, for another endlessly bleak night.

As he reached the door, she cried out, "Leonid!"

He stiffened, as if her voice was an arrow that had hit him between the shoulder blades. Then he turned, his movement reluctant, his gaze apprehensive.

"I thought I could go on like this," she choked. "But I can't. You never gave me a straight answer and I have to have one. However terrible it is, it will be far better than never knowing for sure where we stand and why, and going nuts forever wondering."

In response, there it was again, that corrosive, devouring longing in his eyes.

"You can't keep looking at me like that! Not when you never let me know what it means!"

He only squeezed his eyes shut. But it was too late. She'd seen that look, could no longer doubt what it was.

Her voice rose to a shriek. "If you want your daughters to have a mother and not a wreck, you must put me out of my misery. Tell me what the *hell* is going on."

His gaze lowered, and she thought he'd escape her again, leaving her to go insane with speculation.

Then he raised his gaze and she saw it. The severe aversion to coming clean. And his intention to do it. At last.

Still saying nothing, he walked toward her. But instead of stopping, he bypassed her. Feeling like a marionette, she followed him until he reached the master bedroom.

After closing the door behind them, he half turned to her. "There's something I need to...show you."

Then he started to strip.

Her stupefaction wavered into deeper bewilderment when she realized he wasn't exactly stripping. Turning sideways, brow knotted, face darkened with pain-laced consternation, he left his shirt on, took off his shoes, his belt, undid his zipper, let his pants drop before kicking them away.

Straightening, he finally turned to face her.

But long before he had, with each inch he exposed, her confusion had turned to shock, then to horror.

One of his legs was a map of livid, hideous scars, where massive tissue had been lost, where fractured bones had torn through muscles and shredded skin, and surgeries had put it all back in a horribly disfigured whole.

His other leg was...gone.

Nine

His leg.

Leonid had lost his leg.

In its place, there was a midthigh prosthesis with a facade that resembled his previously normal leg, looking even more macabre than his remaining, mutilated one for it.

All the instances she'd noticed his difficulties in moving, his discomfort, his pain, came crashing back, burying her in an avalanche of details. Then the wheel of memory was yanked to a stop before spooling back at a dizzying speed to that time in his hospital room. New explanations to his every word and glance, making such perfect sense now with hindsight, thudded into place, decimating everything she'd thought she'd known, until she felt everything in her brain falling in a domino effect.

The wheel shot forward through time again, to

the moment he'd reappeared in her life. The way he'd avoided coming near. Stepped away every time she had. Their time on the jet, undoing his clothes only enough to release himself. Not lying down with her, so she wouldn't find out.

But she should have.

Nausea welled, the bile of recriminations filling her up to her eyes. That she hadn't even suspected the significance of what she'd noticed, what she'd felt from him, that she'd been so disconnected from him, so wrapped up in her own suffering and loss, she hadn't felt his.

Every thought and feeling she'd had, toward him, about him, built on that obliviousness, came back to lodge in her brain like an ax, shame hacking at her.

But it wasn't only because he'd lost a limb. Leonid's loss cut so much deeper than that. His legs, both of them, had been more than a vital part of his body. He'd used them like so few on the planet ever had, turning them through discipline and persistence into supreme instruments, catapulting himself to an almost superhuman level of physical prowess and achievement.

But—oh, God—he hadn't only lost his supremacy, he'd lost the ability to walk and run like any other average human being.

And she hadn't been there for him. He'd been alone through the loss and the struggle back to his feet. Such as they were.

Now he was reversing the painfully stilted process of exposing his loss to her, putting his pants and shoes back on, the difficulty with which he found something so simple shredding her heart to smaller pieces. And that was when she was still shell-shocked. When it all sank in, it would tear her apart.

Not that what she felt mattered. Only he did.

Numb with agony, mind and soul in an uproar, she watched him as he walked to the room's sitting area, his every step now taking on a whole new meaning and dimension. Reaching the couch by the balcony with her favorite view of the grounds and the sea, he sank down as if he could no longer stand.

When he finally raised his eyes to her, they were totally empty, like they'd been when he'd first come back.

"That's your answer, Kassandra. From the look on your face, it's even more terrible than anything you've imagined."

Fighting the muteness to contradict his catastrophically inaccurate analysis, she choked, "It's...not...not..."

"Not terrible?" His subdued voice cut across her failed efforts to put what raged inside her into words. "There's no need to placate me, Kassandra. I know exactly how my legs...my *leg*...and the prosthesis look. They're both right out of a horror movie, one from a Frankenstein-like one, the other a Terminator-like one. It's perfectly normal you're appalled."

Objections burst out of her, her anguish at the way he perceived his injuries, her indignation that he thought the way they looked was what horrified her. But they only sounded in her mind. Out loud, she couldn't say one word.

Keeping his dejected gaze fixed on her no doubt stricken one, he exhaled as he heaved up again. "Now you've had your answer, I hope everything is settled."

Her muteness shattered. "Settled? Settled how? You think showing me this answered anything?"

His teeth made a terrible sound. He said nothing.

More realizations bombarded her. "Was that why?

Why you broke it off with me in the past, why you didn't take me up on my offer now? For God's sake, Leonid, why?"

"What do you mean, why? I just showed you."

"I see no answers here. Absolutely none. What do your injuries and loss have to do with anything between us?"

He looked away, as if to hide his response to her feverish response. She teetered up to her feet, approached him. Her heart broke into tinier pieces as he pulled farther away, as if unable to bear her proximity, guarding against her possible touch.

She stopped advancing, stood trembling from head to toe. "If you think you've given me an answer, *the* answer, all you've done is give me more maddening questions. So just tell me, Leonid. Everything since the accident. *Please*."

He appeared about to evade her again, then she sensed something crumbling inside him. That…dread of laying everything inside him bare before her.

Heading back to the couch, he sat down heavily. Wincing, supersensitive to his every move more than ever, she followed him, sat far enough away to give him the space he needed.

Then he talked. "Everything started *before* the accident. While I was training, I realized our arrangement had only been satisfactory because we were together almost every day. Being apart from you made me realize I wanted to be with you, all the time, all my life. I wasn't sure if you felt the same, but I was going to risk it. I was going to propose."

She'd thought she was now prepared for anything he'd say, would hold it together no matter what he threw at her. But this confession made her collapse back on the couch in a nerveless heap.

His expression blipping momentarily at her reaction, he went on. "Even if you'd said no, I'd have waited until you one day wanted me enough or trusted me enough, if that was the issue, to change your mind. But before I could, the accident happened. Then you came to me.

"I'd just been told my legs were beyond salvaging. I also had a spinal injury, and they thought I'd suffer severe erectile dysfunction or even total impotence."

Falling deeper into shock, every second brought her more proof the past two years had been built on misconceptions and ignorance. She'd known nothing of the life-uprooting blows he'd suffered, and he had chosen to suffer alone.

Oh, God, Leonid.

"I was agonized I'd never be a competitive athlete again, would at best rehabilitate enough to walk with a minimum of pain. But what devastated me most was knowing I'd never be the man you'd wanted so fiercely, and had taken such pleasure in."

Before she could cry out that she would want him whatever happened, his next words made her see how he would have never believed it, how he'd convinced himself of the opposite.

"But I knew you were noble, and if you knew, even when it repulsed and horrified you, you wouldn't leave me. I couldn't have you stay with me out of pity. I couldn't saddle you with an impotent cripple. I would have been worse than useless to you, a constant source of unhappiness. I knew even if I was selfish and terrified enough that I clung to you, I'd lose you anyway, when the reality of my situation drove you away in disgust or crushed you in despair.

"I decided to drive you away, without letting you even doubt my prognosis, thought it better to do it at once, rather than in a slow and far more mutilating ordeal. But I didn't expect you to make it that hard. You forced me to push you away as viciously as it took for you to leave me, to save yourself.

"Just as I thought I succeeded in setting you free, you told me you were pregnant. I asked if you'd keep the baby, vaguely wishing your pregnancy wouldn't continue somehow, or that you'd maybe consider giving the baby up for adoption, so you'd sever every tie you had to me, so you could restart your life unburdened again."

This. This was it. What she'd gone insane for, the explanation for his sudden cruelty and coldness, what she'd felt had to exist, but had to accept didn't, to her deepening heartache. But it existed. It explained everything and rewrote history. He'd forced himself to hurt her, fearing he'd destroy her if he didn't. He'd loved her so much, he couldn't let her share the bleak fate he'd thought awaited him.

His gaze swept downward, as if he was looking into his darkest days. "The next months were a worse hell than even I'd imagined they would be. The least of it was the anxiety over my impending physical losses. The memory of hurting you became more suffocating as time went by. My sanity became more compromised as I lived in dread that what I'd hoped for you, that you'd move on, would come to pass, and *then* feeling even worse when it didn't, when you had Eva and Zoya and confined your whole life to them.

"After many setbacks, they managed to save one of

my legs, if in the condition you saw. My spinal injury healed without any neurological deficit, and they hoped I wouldn't be impotent. Not that I could test that. All I could do was struggle to heal, physically and psychologically, and cope with my new, severe limitations. And all that time, I watched you and the twins obsessively from afar as you went through everything I should have been there for, alone.

"Then I was back on my feet, real and prosthetic, just in time for Zorya to call me to duty. And though I never dreamed of having anything with you again, I was no longer going to let anything keep me from being there for you, and from serving the family you gave me, the family I never had, and my country.

"But the moment I saw you again, I knew. My potency was more than intact, and the separation and suffering had only left me perpetually, ferociously starving for you. Yet I had to stay away. You deserve better than the disfigured wreck I am now. I...I would have rather had my remaining leg cut off than let you see me this way, and see that look of horror in your eyes. But your anguish and confusion cornered me into showing you. Now you can at least understand, if not forgive, everything I did."

He fell silent, breathing strident, eyes reddened, face clenched as if with fighting against unbearable pain.

She stared at him, paralyzed.

The enormity of what he'd suffered and lost overwhelmed her. And through it all, he'd selflessly, if mistakenly, thought only of her needs, and not his own.

But his last words had been the worst. Along with his irrevocable losses, his self-worth had been shattered.

The tears finally came, pouring out of her very soul as if under pressure.

Grimacing as if she'd stabbed him, he groaned. "*Bozhe moy*, Kassandra, I can't bear your pain, or your pity."

"Pity? *Pity?*"

Finding nothing that could express her outrage at how totally he'd misconstrued her reaction, she charged him, knocking him back on the couch and climbing all over him, trembling hands groping every inch of him, real and replacement. Inert with shock, he lay beneath her as she smothered him in hugs and kisses and drowned him in tears.

"How dare you… How *dare* you think anything you suffered could have burdened me or put me off? How *could* you make that decision for me, deprive me of being there for you through your ordeal? Didn't you realize I would have given anything to be with you at all, let alone in your darkest time? Didn't you realize that whatever you lost only makes every inch of you even more precious to me? If I could give you a limb to restore yours, I wouldn't think twice."

Looking dazed by her fervor, this last bit made him shudder. "Don't say that, *Bozhe moy*, Kassandra, don't…"

"I'll say it because it's true. Because I love you. You are the only man I loved or would ever love."

He looked even more flabbergasted. "How can you love me after what I put you through, no matter the reasons?"

She grabbed his face, forced him to look at her, as if to drive her conviction into his mind. "I now know I must have always felt what's in your heart, never believed what you said in mine. It was what agonized me most, that what I felt and what I thought I knew were such opposites. Your reasons would have been more than enough to forgive you if you'd done much worse that just pushed me away, and thinking it was for my own good."

His breathing, which usually never quickened due to his supreme fitness, came in rapid, ragged wheezes beneath her burning chest. "Kassandra, you don't know what you're saying, you're shocked by what you saw and heard, feeling sorry for me…"

"Oh, my beloved Leo, I do feel sorry, but not only for you, for me, for us. I am crushed with regret, because I wasn't there for you through it all, because you deprived me of you, throwing us both in hell apart. I feel as if my heart is splintering because you deprived yourself of me and my love and support, of our daughters, missed out on having them bless your life and heal your heart during your darkest time, as they would have even before they were born. But I'm not letting you deprive us of each other anymore. Marry me, Leonid, my love, my only love, for real and forever."

His eyes had been reddening more with her every word. But with her last words, his face contorted and air rushed into his chest, as if he'd been drowning and was drawing a lifesaving breath after breaking the surface.

His eyes glittered, but not with the tears she rained over his face. With what she'd thought she'd never see. *His* tears.

"Don't decide anything now, take time to think, wait…"

Her trembling lips silenced his working ones. "You've been making me wait since I first laid eyes on you. Before you let us be together, while we were together, since you pushed me away and since you came back. And I can't wait anymore. I won't, ever again. I will never waste another moment waiting or worrying or doing anything but loving you and being with you."

And his tears flowed. His body shook beneath hers as she cried out, moved beyond endurance, sobs rocking her.

Straining over him, as if she wanted to slip beneath his skin, to hide him under hers, she moaned into his gasping lips, "Stop thinking, stop assuming what's best for me. You are what's best for me. You are everything I ever wanted for myself. Will you give me everything I want? Will you give me yourself?"

His tears flowing faster, his body beneath hers easing toward impending surrender, he said, "But I'm not the man you once loved anymore..."

She pulled back, let him see himself in her eyes, willing everything she felt for him to restore his faith in himself. "You're not. You're better. Far better. Your ordeals have tempered you into the purest, strongest, best form of yourself. I loved the man you were, but when forced to, I could live without him. I can't live without the man you are now."

"It was the inferno of yearning for you." She gazed in confusion down at him and he elaborated. "What tempered me."

"Then, say yes, Leonid. Marry me, be with me, love me and never leave me alone again."

Tears froze in his eyes as his gaze deepened, as if trying to probe her soul, filling with so much vulnerability, disbelief and hesitation she felt she'd burst with it all.

Slowly, conviction seeped in, followed by dawning elation. Then it was as if he was letting her see into *his* soul for the first time, and all she saw there was...love.

God, *so* much love. Adoration.

"Kassandra, *moya lyubov*, my love, if you'll have me, if you'll let me love you for the rest of my life…yes. Yes to anything and everything you want or will ever want."

Flinging herself at him with all her strength, she bombarded him with tear-drenched kisses, reiterating her supplication. "You. You're all I ever wanted or will ever want."

"And you are everything," he pledged as he surrendered to her fervor, his voice as deep as the sea, and as turbulent with fathoms-deep emotion, mirroring what his eyes detailed. "From the moment I first saw you, I was always yours. Even when I believed you'd never be mine again, I remained yours. I would have remained yours forever."

Suddenly everything inside her exploded into a devastating blaze of lust. After this beyond-belief declaration, she felt she'd crumble if he didn't merge them in every way, right now, hard and long and completely.

Shuddering with need, she scrambled off him, tugging him up with her. He followed her silently as she stumbled to bed, stood watching her as she flung herself onto it, searing her with his hunger.

"Love me, Leonid." Her voice was a husky tremolo that fractured with the desperation of her passion. "Now that I know you love me, *show* me."

Groaning, he came down over her, filled her arms, his hands trembling all over her, as if afraid she wasn't real. Her hands shook in turn over his stubble-covered jawline, up the chiseled planes of his divine face until they dipped into his raven-hued hair. Pulling him closer, her desperate lips clamped over his, her tongue restlessly searching their seam. A pained rumble escaped him as his tongue lashed out to snare hers, duel with it.

His rumbles deepened, filling her, shaking her apart; his hands owned her every inch, setting it ablaze. Reaching her buttocks, he squeezed hard, as if trying to bring himself under control.

Needing him to unleash everything inside him, devastate her with it, her thighs fell apart for him, begging his invasion. "Since you took me again, needing you has become agony. Please, do everything to me again."

Groaning, he nodded, snatching her clothes off her burning body. But as she undid his pants, tried to push them down, his teeth clenched, like his hands over hers.

"Don't. I don't want you to see me like that."

She freed her hands from his convulsive grip, grabbed his face, needing him to believe her once and for all. "I already saw you, and it did horrify me, but only to realize the extent of your injury, what you lost, what you're suffering. But for me, the scars and prosthesis are now part of you, and I love and crave all of you. I'll forever feel thankful whenever I look at them and see a reminder that I still have you, that fate didn't take you from me and granted me the miracle of being able to love you and share our daughters and everything I am with you."

Groaning as if in searing pain, he buried kisses in her palms mixed with tears and a litany of her name and *lyublyu tebya*. It was the first time he'd said it. *I love you.*

She drowned him with her reciprocation.

Getting rid of her last shred of clothes, he freed himself and brought her to his daunting hardness. Shaking with the need to impale herself on it, she threw herself over his chest, pushing his jacket off, teeth undoing his shirt, needing his flesh on hers. But he stopped her again.

"Let me pleasure you like that. I did on the jet, didn't I?"

He meant without exposing himself, at all. He didn't want her to see any part of him, probably was concealing other scars.

He was teetering on the edge of control between her thighs, everything about him promising her the explosive pleasure he'd given her before. She only had to say yes and his hot, throbbing girth and length would slam inside her, in that rough, frenzied tempo that had made her orgasm around him repeatedly on the jet before he'd made her come one last time as he'd climaxed deep inside her.

But… "I want you to *love* me this time. With all of you. I want to make love to all of you."

He held her gaze for one last second before capitulating.

Laying her back on the bed, he rose on his knees, started to take off his clothes. She whimpered as each button, each shrug revealed more to her starving eyes.

She'd been wrong. He hadn't just been upgraded; he'd metamorphosed. This was what the next step of evolution had to look like. And there *were* more scars, crisscrossing his chest, running down his arms and abdomen, interrupting the dark, silky patterns adorning his magnificence. And to her, they looked like arcane patterns, bestowed by destiny, marking him as chosen for glory and uniqueness, and were as beautiful and arousing as everything else about him.

Surging up, she traced the scars with worshiping hands and lips, making him shudder harder with every touch and nip. Delighted to discover they were even more sensitive than the rest of him, would amplify his pleasure, she got bolder.

"Kassandra, you're driving me past insanity."

"Just like you do to me. Stop tormenting me and let me see all of you. Now, Leonid."

Naked from the waist up, eyes averted, he stood up and exposed the rest, his movements so reluctant it squeezed her heart with anguish. He hated doing this, was sick with self-consciousness, still unable to believe she wouldn't cringe at his physical damage and deficit. It would have been easier to let him hide from her. But she couldn't. It would only become a barrier.

She was done letting anything come between them.

She lay back, spread herself, gaze devouring him. "Look at me, my love. See how much more arousing I find you now. Every inch of you is stamped with maturity and power, more than ever. The marks of your suffering tell me incredible stories of endurance and persistence. They're like brands of triumph and they only make you more unique to me. Give me everything you are, my darling Leonid."

Exhaling raggedly, he nodded, growled something ferocious at the sight of her spread in surrender before him. Coming down on the bed, he prowled over her like a ravenous tiger, fully exposed, dauntingly engorged. His hands sought her secrets, her triggers. He took her mouth in a rough kiss before he withdrew, his eyes flaring and subsiding like blue infernos.

"Every single inch of you, every word you say, every breath and look—you are an aphrodisiac I could dilute and dispense to the world and cure all sexual dysfunction. Had I suffered from any, you would have cured me."

Unable to hold back anymore, she writhed beneath him, twisted over him. Realizing what she wanted, he reversed their positions, spread himself for her, letting her have his mind-blowing potency where she craved it, in her watering mouth. He let her do everything she wanted to him, explore him with darting tongue and trembling hands, growling his enjoyment of her homage.

"Own me, *moya dorogaya*, take what's always been yours."

Unable to bear the joy of knowing it had been the same for him, that it had to be her and only her, she took it all, roaming his leg, his prosthesis, his potency, all of him.

She wanted to ask him to take his prosthesis off, let her touch what remained of his leg without barriers. But he'd already crossed too many lines to accommodate her need. That had to wait until he had no lingering doubts of how she'd react, or discomforts in exposing the rest of his vulnerabilities to her.

She was lapping his arousal, more rushes of molten agony flooding her core as she wondered how she would accommodate that much demand, when his hands on her shoulders stopped her. She cried out in frustration, only to find herself on her back again. She held out her arms, hurrying him, hands flailing over whatever she could reach of him. Chuckling his gratification at her urgency, he drowned her in a luxurious, tongue-mating embrace, before he suddenly started extricating himself from her clinging limbs. She whimpered, tried to drag him back, but he restrained her hands.

"Patience. This time, I'm doing this right."

She tried to drag him back with her legs. "You did it right the first time and every time. Just do it again."

He bit into one of the thighs clinging to him. "I will do it, again and again. But I want to do something first."

Getting off the bed, he strode out of sight, then suddenly the chamber was plunged in total darkness.

Her heart thudded. Was he still loath to make love to her while she saw all of him? Or maybe now that he *had* let her see all of him, he needed the respite of darkness?

Suddenly silver light engulfed the whole bed. It took her several stunned heartbeats to realize he'd thrown the drapes and inner shutters of the enclosed balcony open to the night sky. The full moon was framed in the middle of the paneled windows. The moonlight was so intense, she could see nothing outside its domain, didn't know where Leonid was now.

"This is how you should be showcased..." She lurched at his bass rasp as he seemed to materialize before her moonstruck eyes, a colossal shadow detaching from the darkness, made of mystery and magic. "A goddess of wanton desires, of rampant pleasures, waiting for worshippers to come pay homage, glowing, ripe, voracious, spellbinding."

She was all that?

She could only murmur, "Look who's talking."

He came into the moon's spotlight, the stark illumination casting harsh shadows over the noble sculpture of his face, turning it from regal to supernatural. His skin and hair glimmered with highlights as he pushed her back on the bed, loomed over her, the full moon blazing at his back, turning him into a magnificent silhouette. Only his eyes caught its silver beams, glowing like incandescent sapphires. She went limp beneath him with the power of it all, the sheer brutal beauty of him, of these moments.

Her chest tightened one last time over the jagged pieces of the past, the terrible memories, before it let them go, then swelled with the new and uncontainable hopes and expectations. Those of having him again. This time, forever.

Crying out, her desperation shattered the last shackle holding him back. He lunged between her eagerly spreading thighs, letting her feel his dominance for a fraught moment.

"Moya boginya..." Gazing into her streaming eyes, calling her his goddess, he plunged inside her with one long, hard thrust.

Her body jerked beneath him as the hot, vital glide of his thick, rigid shaft in her core drove her into profound sensual shock. She clamped her legs around him, high over his back, giving him full surrender, delirious with witnessing the pleasure of possessing her seizing his face. He ground deeper into her until his whole length was buried inside her, filling her beyond capacity. Sensation sharpened, shattering her. She cried out again, tears flowing faster.

He started moving, severing eye contact only to run fevered appreciation over her body, watching her every quake and grimace of pleasure, all the while growling driven, tormenting things.

"How could there be wanting like this...pleasure like *this*?"

She keened as he accentuated every word with a harder thrust. He devoured the explicit sounds, his tongue invading her mouth, mimicking his body's movements inside her.

Her sanity burned with the friction and fullness of his flesh in hers, the fusion, the totality of it, now that she knew it was indeed total, and would never end.

Her cries grew louder as his plunges grew longer,

until she clawed at him for the jarring rhythm that would finish her. Only then did he build to it, his eyes burning, his face taut, savage with need, sublime in beauty. She fought back her own ecstasy, greedy for the moment his seized him.

Realizing she was holding back, he growled, "Come for me, *moya koroleva*, let me see what I do to you."

Her body almost erupted hearing him call her *my queen*.

But she held on, thrashed her head. "Come with me..."

Roaring, he thrust deeper, destroying her restraint. Release buffeted her, razing her body in convulsions. Those peaked to agony when he succumbed to her demand, gave her what she always craved. Him, at the mercy of the ecstasy of union with her, pleasure racking him, his seed filling her in hard jets. She felt it all, and shattered.

Time and space vanished as he melted into her, grounded the magic into reality, eased her back into her body.

Everything came back into jarring focus when he tried to move off her. She caught him. His weight should have been crushing, but it had always been only anchoring, necessary. Like he was.

But he'd never let her have his weight as long as she wished, insisting it burdened her. He now rose on outstretched arms, his eyes gleaming satisfaction over her ravished state.

"Koroleva moyey zhizhni." He trailed a gently abrasive hand over her, eyes worshipping. "Queen of my life."

A vast thankfulness expanded inside her so hard,

she could barely speak. "How do you say 'king of my world'?"

His whole face blazed with pleasure and pride, his drawl painfully sexy and harsh with emotion. *"Korol' moy mir."*

"Korol' moy mir."

Whispering the pledge against his lips, she could say no more as perfect peace, for the first time in her life, dragged her into a well of contentment where nothing else existed...

Live classic Zoryan music woke Kassandra from a delicious dream filled with Leonid.

The royal band was rehearsing in the seafront gardens again for the coming ceremonies.

Though the drapes were securely drawn, and the chamber was dark, she just knew. The sun was shining today.

It had been shining the past two weeks. Everyone she met insisted it was the blessing of the new king and his twin stars. Kassandra was ready to believe it. If happiness like this was possible, then maybe it bent the very laws of nature to itself, too.

It had changed *her* on a fundamental level. Her heart beat to a different rhythm, her skin had a richer texture, colors had magical hues and life tasted and smelled of him.

Leonid.

Even if she was back in her quarters, and he hadn't been sleeping beside her this past week, practically had no time for her at all in his consuming preoccupation with preparations, she felt him all around her.

And as if he hadn't been insanely busy enough, he

was now preparing living quarters for *them*, not his or the ones she was currently staying in, but something totally new and theirs, now that their marriage would be real.

She'd refused to even see where it would be, wanted him to surprise her. Even as a designer, her imagination could never match what his love would bestow on her.

Now he was running against time so it would be ready on the day of the combined rituals: his coronation, and their wedding.

God...their wedding!

She still couldn't believe any of this was happening.

When she'd asked him to marry her, she'd thought they'd elope, since they'd told everyone they were already married. But Zorya's newly reformed royal council wouldn't sanction an undocumented marriage as proof of the twins' legitimacy. Leonid had said if she hadn't proposed that night, he would have the next morning. Zorya was demanding a wedding to fix their lack of documentation. And from what she was seeing, it was going to be the royal wedding of the century. Her family, who would come two days before the rituals, were all beside themselves with excitement. Yes, even her father.

Everything felt like a fantasy. Far better than one. She constantly found herself wondering if she was having a ridiculously extravagant wish-fulfillment dream and would wake up to the bleak reality of two weeks ago.

Could everything really be this perfect?

Suddenly, her heart contracted with foreboding.

Pausing until the spasm passed, she wondered at the far stronger than usual attack. Seemed the approaching ceremonies and the superstitious bent of this land had her spooked.

Pushing the ridiculous and unfounded anxieties away, she rose and rushed through getting ready.

Hurrying to the girls first, her mood soared again as they concluded their morning rituals. Afterward, she left them with Despina and Anya and went in search of Leonid. Though she'd been leaving him alone to take care of his endless details, she had to see him today. Just touch and kiss him, before leaving him to his urgent affairs.

As she reached his stateroom, Fedor informed her that Leonid had a surprise visit from an important royal family member.

Before she told Fedor to ask Leonid to touch base with her when he could as she didn't want to call and disturb him, the door opened, and what she thought a Valkyrie would look like walked out. And it was clear she was not happy.

Suddenly, Leonid appeared after the woman, and the expression on his face froze her heart. He looked… pained.

The woman turned to him and they shared a charged moment. She was clearly angry. He appeared to be doing all he could to placate her.

Refusing his efforts, the mystery statuesque blonde turned away, leaving him looking more distressed. In a minute she passed Kassandra as she stood in the shadows. Surprise flickered in the woman's eyes before she impaled her on a glance of hostility and walked away.

Leonid just then noticed her and rushed to her, his expression trying to warm, and failing.

Heart thudding, she asked, "Anything wrong?"

He waved. "A trivial dispute. Olga already doesn't approve of my policy making. She'll come around."

Then, kissing her, he promised he'd be there for dinner as usual, excused himself and rushed away.

After watching him until he disappeared, she walked back slowly, wrestling with tremors all the way back to her quarters. It had to be that time of the month making her morose, making her find normal things distressing.

But...if this was normal, why had Leonid lied?

For she had no doubt that he had.

Was there anything else he could have lied about? Like the reason he hadn't been sleeping with her since they'd announced their coming wedding ten days ago?

Had her intuition that nothing could be this perfect been right?

As the girls received her with their usual fanfare, she tried to shake those insidious, malignant doubts.

But they'd already taken root.

Ten

"I so hope Princess Olga will get over her disappointment soon."

Kassandra's hands froze over the gold-and-black costumes she'd designed for Eva and Zoya for the ceremonies.

Anya's words brought images of the incredibly beautiful and regal Olga assailing her. Standing toe-to-toe with Leonid, looking like his female counterpart, every line in her majestic body taut with emotion.

Did Olga's disappointment have to do with Leonid's impending wedding to her? Was that why she'd shot her that antagonistic look? Was she what stood between Olga and the man she wanted?

Forcing herself to sound normal, she asked, "Disappointment over what?"

"That she won't be queen."

That was the first time she'd heard that. No one around here, including Leonid, had told her the details of what had led to him being announced the future king. Even in the news, when other candidates were said to exist, they were never named, since Leonid was the only one who mattered, the one with the global fame and clout.

"So she was one of the candidates for the throne?"

Anya, who Leonid had appointed as her lady-in-waiting, nodded. "She was actually the preferred one. Not only has Zorya always preferred female monarchs, since its birth at the hands of a queen and under the mantle of two goddesses, but Olga is the spitting image of Esfir, Zorya's founder and first queen. Many believe she's her reincarnation."

Kassandra's heart started to thud. "So what happened?"

Oblivious to her condition, Anya handed her another needle threaded with the last color Kassandra needed to finish embroidering Zorya's emblem on Eva's skirt.

"Prince Leonid was always the better candidate, logically speaking, outstripping Olga, and anyone in Zorya for that matter, in wealth and influence by light years. But everyone in Zorya would have overlooked all that because of Olga answering Zorya's specific criteria better. We are a land steeped in tradition and legend, and our beliefs in what makes us Zoryan rule supreme. Olga was an omen, representing our founding queen, a return to the glory days, a rebirth. But *then* Prince Leonid produced something even better. Nonidentical twin daughters, the very personification of our patron goddesses. That made the scale crash in his favor. The representatives of the people and the new royal council were unanimous that it was a sign from the fates. You, my lady, naming them both names meaning *life*, heralding a new life for the kingdom, was, as you Americans say, the cherry on top."

Kassandra tried not to stare at Anya as if she'd just shot her. But the woman's next words felt like more bullets.

"Before Prince Leonid announced the existence of the royal twins and his marriage to you, Princess Olga's supporters advised her to marry him, so Zorya would have him and his power as the queen's consort. So you can understand her disappointment that she not only won't have the title, but won't have the best man on earth as a husband. I only hope she gets over her displeasure and starts collaborating with Prince Leonid. Zorya needs them both."

Three hours and endless details later, Anya left her only when the girls' costumes were done.

Still in an uproar over the revelations, which Leonid hadn't once hinted at, Kassandra continued her efforts to distract herself, now having the girls try on the costumes they'd just finished.

Looking at her daughters in the ornate dresses she'd designed to reflect their new home's history, their new roles as the kingdom's icons, she couldn't help but believe they were born to wear them, to be princesses, with a legacy rooted in tradition and legend.

No wonder the people whose beliefs were based on the lore of the two goddesses thought them a sign from the fates.

But those same people bowed to tradition so much, they'd still refused to sanction such signs' legitimacy based on an undocumented marriage, and had demanded a new wedding. That had been what Kassandra wanted most in life. To marry her beloved Leonid on the same day he became king.

At least, it was what she'd wanted until a few hours ago.

But now...now...she didn't know what to think.

Actually, she did know. And it was...terrible.

If Leonid had needed Eva and Zoya to win the race for the crown, if this is why he'd come for them, it changed everything.

It meant he hadn't come back for them as his daughters. He'd only needed them as his ace, which would trump anyone else's claim, even the preferred heir. But what about her?

Had everything that had happened between them been second to attaining his goal? Was he now marrying her because it was the one way to seal the deal? Or was it far worse than that?

Could it be Olga had always been his preferred choice, but he wouldn't accept anything less than being king himself, with her by his side as his queen consort? Could Kassandra be simply the more convenient choice, a means to make the best of a terrible situation, since he adamantly believed that he and the girls were what was best for the kingdom?

Could he be that driven to become king, over anybody's hearts and lives, including his own? Could it be all that passion, all those emotions, all the things he'd told her, had all been him doing whatever it took to fulfill his duty, to claim his destiny?

From then on her projections grew even more morbid. Maybe he was biding his time until after the coronation and the wedding, when his need for her would end, so he could leave her for the woman he wanted for real.

If so, was what he'd told her that day in his hospital room the truth after all? That he'd never cared for her, hated her clinging and couldn't wait to be rid of her?

It all made sense in a macabre way. For if it didn't, why had he come back for the girls, and according to him for her, too, only when Zorya had announced its secession and its revival of the monarchy? Why hadn't he told her anything about Olga or his need for the girls to secure the throne before? Was he really as preoccupied as he appeared, or was he only unable to feign desire for her anymore?

If *any* of that was real, how could she go through with the wedding? How could she give him every right to the girls?

If any of those horrible suspicions were true, it made him a monster.

"Yes, sir, I understand."

This statement, or variations of it, had been all that Leonid got to say for the past half hour, as Kassandra's father gave him a winded lecture, liberally peppered with ill-veiled threats, about manhood, marriage and family life.

At least it seemed his total submission to the man's badgering and his unqualified acceptance of his menacing directives appeased the proud and forceful Greek man. Now Leonid decided to put his mind to rest completely.

"I assure you, Kyrie Stavros, I left Kassandra only because I thought my life was over after the accident, and I believed it was for the best not to tie her life, and the twins', to someone as damaged as I was. But I've since been restored more than I dreamed possible, and Kassandra, and Eva and Zoya, have completed my healing. Kassandra is my heart, my everything, and I'd give my life without a second thought to never hurt her again. I *will* give my life to make her happy."

Loukas Stavros's eyes had widened with every word, seemingly impressed by Leonid's impassioned declaration, which he clearly hadn't expected.

Reeling back his surprise, Stavros tried to pin austerity back on his face. "As long as we understand each other."

Fiercely glad that Kassandra, and the twins, had such a man, such a family to love and protect them so fiercely, Leonid's lips spread in a grin. "We certainly do. And thanks for your restraint. If it was me talking to the man who left either Eva or Zoya pregnant and heartbroken, I would have taken him apart first, *then* given him the lecture."

The man flung his arms at him in a see-what-I-mean gesture. "I told her that! But she threatened she'd ban me from ever entering Zorya if I didn't give my word to take it easy on you!"

Leonid laughed, his gaze seeking Kassandra. His golden goddess was fierce in her protectiveness of him.

Finding her nowhere, he turned his attention to Stavros. "That sounds very much like our indomitable Kassandra. I'm only glad you complied so you can attend the wedding, and give her away as is your, and her, right. But if you want to discipline me afterward, I'm at your service."

The man gave him an excited wolflike grin. "It seems you and me are going to get along, boy."

Leonid grinned back at him as widely. "I have no doubt we will. I would get along with the devil if he loved and cherished Kassandra. But as my father-in-law, and my daughters' grandfather, you automatically commanded privileges few in this world do. Now after meeting you, you've just moved to the top of my list."

Stavros laughed. "The list of devils?"

Leonid winked at him. "I do have a weakness for my kind."

Stavros guffawed louder and thumped him on the back so hard he almost knocked him off his unsteady feet.

By the time Stavros moved on, the demonstrative man had inundated him with enough physical gestures to tell him he was already family to him.

Relieved that he'd won over the most important man in Kassandra's life, Leonid turned to the other people who sought his attention at the reception, all the while seeking Kassandra, to no avail.

The coronation, and more important, the wedding, was tomorrow, and her whole family, all two-hundred-plus members of it, had arrived in Zorya the day before. She'd been lost in their sea ever since. Not that she'd been easily found before that. In the two weeks after they'd come together, he'd almost killed himself to wrap a million things up so he could rush back into her arms. But once he could, there had always been something stopping her from taking him there. For the past week she'd either been busy, sleeping, out or just unavailable when he'd sought her.

Even when he did see her, he couldn't help but notice she'd...changed. She was subdued, as if all her fire had gone out. She'd only told him she had her period, and it was a particularly distressing one, what with all the preceding events.

But when he'd thought they'd go to meet her arriving family members together, and she'd gone alone, all his past doubts had crashed back on him.

For what if, after the first rush of sympathy for what had happened to him, it had all sunk in, that she'd be tying herself to a man who wasn't only damaged, and who in spite of her protestations, she found revolting, but who would be the king of a country passing through turbulent times for the foreseeable future? What if she dreaded all the tension and trouble he would bring into her own life by association?

But though it agonized him to think any of that could be true, he dreaded saying anything to her even more, in case she validated his suspicions. So he'd chosen to convince himself she'd been having wedding jitters, that whatever it was, it was a passing thing that had nothing to do with him, or their impending marriage.

But when the reception ended, and she'd reappeared only to entertain her guests while keeping dozens of feet and people between them, he could no longer fool himself.

Something was wrong. Horribly wrong.

Three hours before the coronation and wedding ceremonies, Leonid stood before the full-length mirror in the quarters he'd relinquish forever tonight to move with Kassandra to the ones he'd slaved over realizing for her, her perfect wonderland.

His traditional Zoryan regal costume fit him perfectly. And weighed down on him absolutely. But he realized it wasn't the lifelong responsibility it represented that was getting him down, but the hovering dread that he wouldn't be bearing its burdens with a happy Kassandra by his side.

Then, as if he'd summoned her with his anxiety, Kassandra entered his quarters.

Just one look into her extinguished eyes told him.

His worst fears were about to be realized.

Forcing himself to ignore his trepidations, he rushed to take her in his arms. His heart almost ruptured when the woman who'd dissolved with passion in his arms a couple of weeks ago turned to stone there now. When she was supposed to walk down the aisle with him to a lifetime together in mere hours.

Before he could choke out his anguish, she whispered, "In spite of everything that happened, and how you came back into our lives, I believe you now love our daughters."

Confused beyond words at hers, he again tried to reach for her. "Kassandra, *moya lyubov'*…"

Her hand rose, a feeble move without any energy. It still stopped him in his tracks. "I also do believe you'd make Zorya the best king. So for our daughters and for your kingdom, I'll walk out there in three hours and marry you, Leonid. But for myself, I want things to go back to what you intended before. A marriage in name only, with separate lives."

Feeling his world coming to an end, he couldn't even breathe for long moments until he thought he might suffocate.

It was finally uncontainable agony that forced the choking question from his lips. "What changed?"

"Nothing changed. Things only became clear."

He squeezed his eyes, his whole left side going numb.

Things were clear to her now. When he'd been trying to cling to the hope that she'd never come to her senses.

"It's too much for you, isn't it?" he rasped. "You tried to pretend my mutilation doesn't appall you, but it does, doesn't it? You can't face a lifetime of curbing your revulsion at the sight of my stump, to the feel of my scars, can you?"

Her gaze deadened even more. "You can pick whatever reason you want. I'll back up any story you decide on."

"Story?"

"If you ever need grounds for divorce."

With that, she turned and walked out, looking like an automaton.

But somewhere in the tornado that was uprooting everything inside him, he knew. She was now going to put on her wedding dress, then she'd walk with him to the altar, pledge to be his wife and queen, and instead of love and joy, he'd see in her eyes that she no longer wanted him. But out of duty to her daughters and their kingdom, she would still walk into the prison of being with him forever.

He couldn't let her do this to herself.

He had to set her free, forever this time.

Shattered by her brief yet annihilating confrontation with Leonid, Kassandra had gone back to her quarters, where all the women of her family had gathered. In a fugue, she surrendered to their fussing as they dressed her in the fairy-tale dress Signor Bernatelli had designed for her. She thought she'd talked, smiled, even laughed, putting on a show for her family's sake, for Eva's and Zoya's, for Zorya's.

After her suspicions about Leonid's intentions had

erupted, wiping out her sanity, they'd receded enough to make her see the facts. That Leonid did love Eva and Zoya, with everything in him, and they loved him back. He was everything they could have hoped for in a father. Also undeniable was the fact that he was a formidable force for good, and as Zorya's king, he would not only save the kingdom, but he'd stabilize the whole region.

As for his feelings for her, whatever he'd felt before, she now believed he was trying sincerely to be as attentive and loving as he could be. In the past week, he'd resumed seeking her, yet it had been as if it hurt him to do so.

Whatever it was, it wasn't as sinister as she'd thought in that first wave of insanity. He was trying to do his best for all of them. It was she who was too greedy, too damaged. She couldn't take what he was offering, when it was far more than what most women could dream of. Because it wasn't everything. She'd either have all of him, or none of him at all.

In keeping with tradition, everyone left her for one last hour of solitude before the wedding. As the minutes counted down to zero, she waited to be called when the ceremonies began.

Then Anya walked in, looking stricken.

"My lady, it's terrible. An absolute shock!"

Kassandra shot to her feet, her blood not following her up, making her sway. "What happened?"

"Prince Leonid has left the palace. After calling Princess Olga and relinquishing the crown to her!"

Among the total mayhem Leonid's departure had caused, Kassandra clung to one thing.

The letter he'd left her.

Not that she'd even tried to read it. His actions had spoken far louder than anything he could ever say. That she'd catastrophically and unforgivably misjudged his feelings and misread his intentions. Again.

She'd exploded from the palace in search of him five hours ago. She'd taken Fedor and he'd driven her to every single place he could think of where Leonid might be. Leonid had turned off his phone, hadn't been anywhere they'd searched. There'd been no sighting of him anywhere. Yet there was no evidence that he'd left the kingdom.

After the last failed attempt, she broke down and wept until she felt she'd come apart. But she got out his letter, hoping it would give her a clue where he'd gone.

Shaking so hard, eyes so swollen, it was almost impossible to read it. But she kept trying.

And every word killed her all over again.

Kassandra,

I will never be able to beg your forgiveness enough or atone enough for everything I cost you, every heartache I caused you, but I'll make sure you never again sacrifice your well-being and desires for anything, starting with me. I will always love you, and our daughters. You will all, always, have everything that I have. But I only want you to be free and happy. While I will always be infinitely grateful for all the happiness and blessings you've given me, I only wish I could take back the suffering I've inflicted on you. But since I can't, I can only cause you no more.

The letter ended, no signature, no closing, just this ominous pledge. The whole message sounded like… like a…

No. No. *No.*

Then it erupted in her mind. A memory. A realization. Of the only place he could be. *Had* to be. One with significance only to him, where he'd taken her and the girls, saying it had been his favorite spot when he'd been a child. The one memory he had of his parents, where they'd taken him right before they died.

Crying out for Fedor to find it, knowing just a name and a description, it felt like forever before Fedor found out where it was. All that time terror hacked at her, that she might have pushed him into doing something drastic.

Then they were there…and…so was Leonid.

He stood in the distance, looking over the frozen lake where his parents had taken him skating for the first, and last, time. A colossus among the snow, looking desolate, defeated.

"Leonid!"

He jerked so hard at her shriek. He must have been so lost in thought that he hadn't heard the car's approach. He almost lost his balance as he swung around. Then he gaped.

She knew how she must look to him. Maniacal, her elaborate wedding gown tearing in places, hair falling all over out of its chignon, eyes reddened and bleeding mascara, the rest of her makeup streaked down her swollen face.

She only cared that she'd found him. That she'd give her life to make it up to him, that she still had the chance to.

When she was a few dozen feet away, he started talking, voice hoarse and even deeper than usual with bleakness. "You shouldn't have come, Kassandra. I meant every word, that only your happiness and peace of mind matter to me."

She would have closed those final feet between them in a flying leap that landed her against him. The old Leonid would have caught her midair as easily as a pro basketball player caught a ball. But as it was, she could knock him off his feet or even injure him. She'd done enough of that, and she'd die before she hurt him again.

"I don't want you to feel bad," he choked. "It's not your fault…"

And she wrapped her arms around as much of his bulk as she could, squeezed him until she felt her arms would break off.

Stiffening as if with insupportable pain in her arms, he groaned in protest again. "Don't, Kassandra. Don't let your tender heart overrule your best interests again. I don't matter…"

"Only you *ever* mattered." She shut him up when he attempted to protest, surging for his precious lips, taking them in wrenching kisses, pouring her love and agony into him. Then she told him what she'd learned that day from Anya, and how it had set off the chain reaction of uncertainty.

"I've lived with the demons of doubt tormenting me for so long," she sobbed in between desperate kisses. "And they overwhelmed my reason. I was terrified you couldn't possibly love me as totally as I love you, that I couldn't be your one and only choice, and that you were only struggling to accommodate my emotions to make the best of a less-than-ideal situation for all involved. And once I thought that, I couldn't do this to you, couldn't bear having you on those terms." Tears poured thicker, sobs coming harder as she mashed her lips against his. "Please forgive me, my love, forgive me for letting malignant insecurity drive me insane enough to commit the unforgivable crime of doubting you again."

As he started to push away, to get a word in, she clung harder, sobs dismantling her soul as she rushed on to confess her original sin.

"I should have *never* walked away when you asked me to. I *knew* you were at your lowest, *knew* you couldn't be in your right mind. Your decision to push me away for my own good was wrong. But the blame for everything that happened is mine, for not insisting on staying, taking anything from you, until you realized I'd a million times rather be miserable with you than at peace without you. I'm the one who made us all suffer."

"Now, wait a minute here…"

She cut across his protest. "No more waiting. And no more doubts or distance of any sort, ever again. I'm never leaving your side again. And I'm *not* letting you relinquish the crown."

"Kassandra, listen to me…"

"No, you listen. I'm not letting you even think of abandoning something this enormous and imperative, your duty to the land only you can rule."

"If you'll just let me get a word in here…"

"What word would that be? If it's not yes to everything I've just said, don't bother. Zorya needs you as much as I and the girls do." She stopped, grimaced. Every cell hurt with loving him so much, finding him so damned beautiful. "Okay, so that's not true. Anyone else, even the girls, can live without you. I can't. And I never will. I need you to believe this, my love, and understand it as a fundamental fact of my being. For the girls, my family and work, I can exist, appear to be functioning, for a lifetime if need be. But to *live*, to know joy and ecstasy and peace, I need you. Only you."

Anguish and insecurity evaporating slowly in his eyes under the flames of her fervor, he caressed her face with trembling hands, the love in his gaze so fierce it seared her to her soul, the raggedness in his deep, velvet voice heart wrenching.

"It was so easy to fall prey to my own demons as soon as I felt your withdrawal. They convinced me I repelled you, and the kingdom's duties and dangers oppressed you. And I would rather die a thousand deaths than inflict a moment's unhappiness on you. But without you fueling my will to be, nothing else mattered. Leaving everything behind became the only thing I could do, and my one desire."

Before she could lament a protest, his lips shook in a smile of reassurance. "But Olga will make a fine queen. And with you by my side again, I can again function, can serve Zorya as her advisor, as a businessman and politician. But it is better for our family that I step down now."

"If you're referring to those moronic fears I had at the start, please forget I ever said anything so stupid. Whatever hardships will be involved in reestablishing the monarchy, this is your *destiny*. I will eagerly and proudly share in all its tests and burdens, and be the happiest woman on earth, because I will do it all with you, and will have the honor and delight of being your succor and support through it all."

And she felt it, the exact moment he let go of the last traces of reluctance and doubt and hesitation. Then she was in the only home she ever wanted, his embrace, crushed and cherished and contained.

"You've got one thing wrong, *dorogaya*. The crown isn't my destiny. You are. You and our girls." Suddenly he groaned. "But how can I now go back and demand to be crowned? After I left the whole kingdom in the lurch?"

Caressing his chiseled cheek dreamily, she sighed. "Don't you worry. Everything about you is the stuff of fairy tales, and when I'm finished playing the media, the whole world will be raving about the king who started his rule with a romantic gesture for the ages. Bet you will go down history as a legend to rival that of the goddesses or even Cinderella and Prince Charming."

His breathtaking smile singed her to her toes. "You mean *we* will. Even though the roles were embarrassingly reversed here, and it was the big, lethal hero who ran away."

A laugh bubbled from her depths. "Leaving me a priceless letter instead of a glass slipper."

His eyes glowed with so much love it caused a literal pain in her gut. "And you didn't send people to look for me, but cast out your love like a net to find me."

Suddenly a storm of honking erupted, jogging them out of their complete absorption with one another.

Swinging around in shock, they found their whole wedding party, six-hundred-plus strong, descending from a fleet of limos. Fedor must have reported their position. Or her testosterone tribe had followed her GPS signal. Or her friends had had their Triumvirate comb the planet for them.

Whatever had really happened, they'd found them and were advancing on them en masse. In the first line of the approaching army were her parents, each with a girl yelling for Kassandra and Leonid in their arms.

Before they reached them, she looked up at Leonid, her soul in human form, the source of every towering emotion she'd ever experienced and the fuel for every ambition and passion and delight for the rest of her life. He was looking back at her, so hungrily, so adoringly, she again wondered how she could have ever doubted his feelings. But never again.

Heart soaring with all the endless possibilities and promises of a lifetime with him, she suddenly grinned at him.

"How about you demonstrate one of your unique abilities to the good people who came trudging through the snow after us?"

His eyes filled with the mischief that had started appearing in his eyes in those short days of bliss, the bliss that would now be their status quo.

"The Voronov Vacuum Maneuver?"

Devouring his lips once again, she caressed his chiseled cheek. "Right the first time."

Laughing, the most delightful sound in heaven or on earth, he opened his arms wide.

The girls launched themselves there, and stuck.

As she explained the property he and the girls, the pieces of her soul, shared, everyone laughed. Then their interrupted wedding guests inundated them with a hundred questions about what was going on.

As they tried to escape answering any, her friends, their Triumvirate and her siblings came to their rescue.

Selene, hooking her arm around her own Greek god, grinned. "You people just have to get used to having a very unconventional, unpredictable king and queen. Don't bother trying to figure them out."

Aristedes grinned adoringly at his wife and corroborated her words. "There's no doubt that under Leonid and Kassandra's rule Zorya will rise to unprecedented prosperity, but it won't be in any way you people would expect. So just sit back and enjoy their reign."

Maksim nodded, grinning, too, as he hugged Caliope to his side. "Now you'll add a new legend to your impressive arsenal, that of The King Who Ran."

Caliope smiled from ear to ear. "And The Queen Who Brought Him Back."

Naomi chuckled. "With yours being a femalecentric culture, that gender-reversal twist on Cinderella and Prince Charming is right up your alley."

Andreas kissed the top of Naomi's head, clearly loving the wit of his wife's remark. "One thing is certain. With those two and their twin stars, I assure you, you'll be forever entertained."

Aleks chuckled. "Indeed. I have a feeling those two will treat us all to lifelong episodes of an epic Greek *and* Slavic–in–one drama. I, for one, can't wait to watch it unfold."

As everyone laughed, Kassandra's eldest brother, Dimitri, who'd spent last night's reception wrapped around Olga, cleared his throat importantly.

"And now I interrupt today's episode with a news bulletin. A message for you, Leonid, from HRH Princess Olga."

As everyone turned to Dimitri, all ears, he smirked.

"The lady is telling you, quote, she'll be your spare heir, until your real ones grow up, but that would be it. You have to get back where you belong, that lofty palace you spent bazillions renovating, put that crown on your head and take the weight of this messed-up kingdom on your endless shoulders. And if you think every time she pinches your ear over some state policy you can flounce away and say you're not playing, you have another think coming, unquote."

Dimitri turned his bedeviling gaze to Kassandra. "*And* she thought you were the reason Leonid was being so uncharacteristically lenient as to approve that policy that made her blast him. But I assured her you're a shark, and that as soon as you knew he didn't use his many rows of teeth when he should have, you'll straighten him, and those teeth, out. And that if she ever needs anything at all done to him, including twisting him into a pretzel, you're the girl to call." He winked broadly at her. "She thinks you'll be her new best friend."

Leonid again laughed along with everyone, unable to believe what a difference an hour made. A minute. A word. Even a breath from Kassandra turned his world upside down, then right side up again.

And she'd given him everything he'd never dared dream of having, dissipating the darkness of despair and insecurity and guilt forever. She'd given him certainty, stability, permanence. She'd taken him and would keep him, no matter what—scars, fake parts, burdens and obsessions and all.

And he finally knew what happiness felt like. And boundless hope. What he'd been scared to even wish for since he'd lost her that first time.

She'd given him everything. And more.

As everyone's voices rose in side conversations and questions and proddings, he was unable to go on another second without another kiss.

Everyone hooted and said they should have brought the minister with them and completed the wedding right here.

Whispering to Kassandra, she just nodded delightedly and said, "Anything you want, always."

He addressed the crowd. "I apologize for the drama I caused, though it seems you all enjoyed the mystery and the exercise. But my queen and bride has decreed we go back and resume the interrupted ceremonies, even if by now they'll be concluded long after the sun of the new day rises. I hope you're all game."

As everyone's voices rose in approval, he squeezed his little princesses, who were beside themselves with the excitement of the unusual circumstances.

"And now it's time your papa took you back to your new home, where you will always be the earthbound Zoryan stars that will guide me with their bright light, and the blessing of our kingdom."

As everyone walked back to the limos, Kassandra, whose tears of joy had been flowing freely, reached for his lips, her voice thick with emotion, sultry with hunger.

"I've got news for you, my liege. After all the odds you've beaten, how you've survived and become far more than you've been, how you've come back for us, how you love us and how you make our lives far better than any dream, the real blessing is you."

He hugged the twins tighter, hugged his Kassandra until he felt her under his skin, inside his heart, coursing through his veins and pledged, "And I am all yours totally, irrevocably…and forever."

* * * * *

If you liked this tale of royalty and romance,
pick up these other stories from
USA TODAY *bestselling author Olivia Gates*

TEMPORARILY HIS PRINCESS
CONVENIENTLY HIS PRINCESS
SEDUCING HIS PRINCESS

Available now from Harlequin Desire!

***

And don't miss the next
BILLIONAIRES AND BABIES *story,*
HIS FOREVER FAMILY
from Sarah M. Anderson
Available February 2016!

***

If you're on Twitter, tell us what you think of
Harlequin Desire! #harlequindesire

MILLS & BOON®
Hardback – January 2016

ROMANCE

The Queen's New Year Secret	Maisey Yates
Wearing the De Angelis Ring	Cathy Williams
The Cost of the Forbidden	Carol Marinelli
Mistress of His Revenge	Chantelle Shaw
Theseus Discovers His Heir	Michelle Smart
The Marriage He Must Keep	Dani Collins
Awakening the Ravensdale Heiress	Melanie Milburne
New Year at the Boss's Bidding	Rachael Thomas
His Princess of Convenience	Rebecca Winters
Holiday with the Millionaire	Scarlet Wilson
The Husband She'd Never Met	Barbara Hannay
Unlocking Her Boss's Heart	Christy McKellen
A Daddy for Baby Zoe?	Fiona Lowe
A Love Against All Odds	Emily Forbes
Her Playboy's Proposal	Kate Hardy
One Night...with Her Boss	Annie O'Neil
A Mother for His Adopted Son	Lynne Marshall
A Kiss to Change Her Life	Karin Baine
Twin Heirs to His Throne	Olivia Gates
A Baby for the Boss	Maureen Child

MILLS & BOON®
Large Print – January 2016

ROMANCE

The Greek Commands His Mistress	Lynne Graham
A Pawn in the Playboy's Game	Cathy Williams
Bound to the Warrior King	Maisey Yates
Her Nine Month Confession	Kim Lawrence
Traded to the Desert Sheikh	Caitlin Crews
A Bride Worth Millions	Chantelle Shaw
Vows of Revenge	Dani Collins
Reunited by a Baby Secret	Michelle Douglas
A Wedding for the Greek Tycoon	Rebecca Winters
Beauty & Her Billionaire Boss	Barbara Wallace
Newborn on Her Doorstep	Ellie Darkins

HISTORICAL

Marriage Made in Shame	Sophia James
Tarnished, Tempted and Tamed	Mary Brendan
Forbidden to the Duke	Liz Tyner
The Rebel Daughter	Lauri Robinson
Her Enemy Highlander	Nicole Locke

MEDICAL

Unlocking Her Surgeon's Heart	Fiona Lowe
Her Playboy's Secret	Tina Beckett
The Doctor She Left Behind	Scarlet Wilson
Taming Her Navy Doc	Amy Ruttan
A Promise...to a Proposal?	Kate Hardy
Her Family for Keeps	Molly Evans

MILLS & BOON®
Hardback – February 2016

ROMANCE

Leonetti's Housekeeper Bride	Lynne Graham
The Surprise De Angelis Baby	Cathy Williams
Castelli's Virgin Widow	Caitlin Crews
The Consequence He Must Claim	Dani Collins
Helios Crowns His Mistress	Michelle Smart
Illicit Night with the Greek	Susanna Carr
The Sheikh's Pregnant Prisoner	Tara Pammi
A Deal Sealed by Passion	Louise Fuller
Saved by the CEO	Barbara Wallace
Pregnant with a Royal Baby!	Susan Meier
A Deal to Mend Their Marriage	Michelle Douglas
Swept into the Rich Man's World	Katrina Cudmore
His Shock Valentine's Proposal	Amy Ruttan
Craving Her Ex-Army Doc	Amy Ruttan
The Man She Could Never Forget	Meredith Webber
The Nurse Who Stole His Heart	Alison Roberts
Her Holiday Miracle	Joanna Neil
Discovering Dr Riley	Annie Claydon
His Forever Family	Sarah M. Anderson
How to Sleep with the Boss	Janice Maynard

MILLS & BOON®
Large Print – February 2016

ROMANCE

Claimed for Makarov's Baby	Sharon Kendrick
An Heir Fit for a King	Abby Green
The Wedding Night Debt	Cathy Williams
Seducing His Enemy's Daughter	Annie West
Reunited for the Billionaire's Legacy	Jennifer Hayward
Hidden in the Sheikh's Harem	Michelle Conder
Resisting the Sicilian Playboy	Amanda Cinelli
Soldier, Hero...Husband?	Cara Colter
Falling for Mr December	Kate Hardy
The Baby Who Saved Christmas	Alison Roberts
A Proposal Worth Millions	Sophie Pembroke

HISTORICAL

Christian Seaton: Duke of Danger	Carole Mortimer
The Soldier's Rebel Lover	Marguerite Kaye
Return of Scandal's Son	Janice Preston
The Forgotten Daughter	Lauri Robinson
No Conventional Miss	Eleanor Webster

MEDICAL

Hot Doc from Her Past	Tina Beckett
Surgeons, Rivals...Lovers	Amalie Berlin
Best Friend to Perfect Bride	Jennifer Taylor
Resisting Her Rebel Doc	Joanna Neil
A Baby to Bind Them	Susanne Hampton
Doctor...to Duchess?	Annie O'Neil

MILLS & BOON®

Why shop at millsandboon.co.uk?

Each year, thousands of romance readers find their perfect read at millsandboon.co.uk. That's because we're passionate about bringing you the very best romantic fiction. Here are some of the advantages of shopping at www.millsandboon.co.uk:

* **Get new books first**—you'll be able to buy your favourite books one month before they hit the shops

* **Get exclusive discounts**—you'll also be able to buy our specially created monthly collections, with up to 50% off the RRP

* **Find your favourite authors**—latest news, interviews and new releases for all your favourite authors and series on our website, plus ideas for what to try next

* **Join in**—once you've bought your favourite books, don't forget to register with us to rate, review and join in the discussions

Visit **www.millsandboon.co.uk**
for all this and more today!